About this book

Inspired By True Events

Two Lives, Separated by Time, Joined by Fate...

Emily and Diane have never met yet they are both connected in some mysterious way, but what is it that will make them fatefully unite? and for all of eternity?

Emily, a young Scottish woman suffers flashbacks of past memories and is haunted by many of her life experiences, some of which she cannot explain due to their otherworldly nature. Emily desperately needs to know why she is here, going through all that she is and what her true purpose really is. Unexpected, explosive events along the way cause an immense change in her life forever. Nothing is the same again. On the other side of the border, Diane, a married doctor, struggles with the intensity that her life brings. Diane is troubled by difficulties within her marriage and personal life. Catastrophic revelations cause her mood and decisions to spiral out of control. But is this what was always meant for her?

What people are saying

It was written with such perfect detail that I could imagine myself being there, the atmosphere, the surroundings. were set so well. With each chapter weaving in and out of Diane and Emily's life, taking me down two different path's I didn't know what would happen next making it an exciting and gripping read that I just couldn't put the book down. This book is a page turner.

Christine J

Loved the intensity of the story, couldn't put the book down, absolutely exciting, thrilling and so captivating. The author has a very unique style of writing, Great read, 5 out of 5
★ ★ ★ ★ ★

A. Cowan

The book left me on edge. Wondering what was going to happen next. Exciting from start to finish. The author was so descriptive and gave so much detail.

Rachel A

This book is a must read. I couldn't wait to find out what was happening with Emily. Katie's writing is so incredibly detailed that it will leave you wanting to dwell into your own past.

About the Author

Katie Johnston always knew she had a spiritual side to her from a very young age, which has since developed incredibly over the years. Her passion now is writing out many of her personal experiences in the hope of being able to give comfort, answers and help to anyone that may need it.

Dedication

To my Mother, Sister, and Daughter. Thank You for always being my hope and strength and forever supporting me in all that I do.

Acknowledgements

I would like to Thank everyone involved in helping make this book go from a dream into a reality. It really is true, something that started out as a hobby, soon became a passion and I will be forever grateful for discovering my life's true purpose through my writing.

Perhaps the biggest gratitude goes to my mum Agnes and my sister Christine Johnston for always being there and lending a gentle and guiding push encompassed with words of support, encouragement, and wisdom when I needed to find courage. Even if it was all hours of the day, thank you to you both for being my biggest supporters and a positive influence throughout the years, I appreciate it more than you will ever know. Thank You to my daughter Portia who has the truest and kindest soul. You changed my life in so many ways, you are my guiding light, my strength, and my determination to keep going no matter what. I love you with all my heart, forever my beautiful girl. Much appreciation also goes to my loyal friends… you all know who you are, never failing to make me laugh and encourage the fun and silly when it was most needed. It has perhaps been all the challenges that life has thrown at me that I should be most grateful for. All of the life lessons, during the hardest, impossibly difficult times. Those times taught me to speak my truth, stand up for myself and others, and to always believe that the impossible is most certainly possible. I believe that sometimes we must suffer in order to become of help to others and helping others is what I vow to do in the best way I can.

To Debbie

I hope you enjoy reading this book! Thank you for being a wonderful friend all these years!

Lots of Love
Katie x

THE PAST SHE LIVES WITH

by Katie Johnston

© 2022

Published by Filament Publishing Ltd
16 Croydon Road, Waddon, Croydon,
Surrey, CR0 4PA, United Kingdom
Telephone +44(0)20 8688 2598
info@filamentpublishing.com
www.filamentpublishing.com

ISBN 978-1-915465-18-4
© 2022 Katie Johnston

The right of Katie Johnston to be identified as the author of this work is asserted by her in accordance with the Designs and Copyright Act 1988.

All rights reserved.
No portion of this work may be copied without the prior written permission of the publishers.

Printed by 4edge Ltd

Table of Contents

CHAPTER ONE
EMILY - THE YOUNG YEARS   13

CHAPTER TWO
EMILY – UNDYING LOVE FOR THE UNKNOWN   18

CHAPTER THREE
EMILY – NIGHT SWEATS   23

CHAPTER FOUR
DIANE – THE GIRL WITH THE GOLDEN HAIR   28

CHAPTER FIVE
DIANE – LULWORTH LOVE   31

CHAPTER SIX
EMILY – REINCARNATION   38

CHAPTER SEVEN
DIANE – COMMITMENT   42

CHAPTER EIGHT
DIANE -THE SHORTEST DAY AFTER THE
LONGEST NIGHT BEFORE   49

CHAPTER NINE
EMILY – ATTRACTION   55

CHAPTER TEN
EMILY – THE DREAM   59

CHAPTER ELEVEN
DIANE – SURPRISES					65

CHAPTER TWELVE
DIANE & EMILY – BEGINNINGS AND ENDINGS	72

CHAPTER THIRTEEN
EMILY – THE MAD, THE UGLY AND THE EVIL	79

CHAPTER FOURTEEN
DIANE – STRANGER TO ME				83

CHAPTER FIFTEEN
EMILY – WONDERS AND WARINESS			94

CHAPTER SIXTEEN
DIANE – WHAT I NEVER KNEW			108

CHAPTER SEVENTEEN
DIANE – ALL YOU CAN DO IS TRY			121

CHAPTER EIGHTEEN
EMILY – SUNSHINE IN THE MORNING		134

CHAPTER NINETEEN
DIANE & EMILY – THE END IS NIGH AND
NIGH IS NOW					144

CHAPTER TWENTY
EMILY & DIANE – ALONE				152

CHAPTER TWENTY-ONE
EMILY & LEWIS - THE MAIN MAN			161

CHAPTER TWENTY-TWO
DIANE & DANIEL – THE END			175

CHAPTER TWENTY-THREE
EMILY – FALLING					189

CHAPTER TWENTY-FOUR
EMILY – DYING TO MOVE ON   200

CHAPTER TWENTY-FIVE
EMILY – THUS SHE   212

CHAPTER TWENTY-SIX
EMILY – SET FREE   225

CHAPTER TWENTY-SEVEN
EMILY – THE END – UPDATE   230

CHAPTER ONE

The Young Years

Yeah, I was out of touch, but it wasn't because I didn't know enough, I just knew too much. Does that make me crazy?

Gnarles Barkley

Emily Prescott

It was August 15^{th,} 2006. I woke up slowly. My final year of school.

I despised the school; it nauseated me in every sense of the word. My thoughts at that moment were that any form of escape from that era of *'disappointment for life',* would have felt like dying and floating away to heaven.

Each day was a slow funeral, spent in constant mourning. The smell and the sounds repeating; the very sight of all those unappealing and naïve academic faces made my stomach churn. I almost felt seasick as the weight of my world pressed down on me and my heart began to race. Suddenly, I felt like I couldn't breathe.

Choking, gasping for air, exasperating.

It was all anxiety in disguise. At no point ever back then, did I completely understand or know what exactly it was that enforced me to hate that place and to endure the anxiety-filled mind state so much. I suppose I was just not cut out for tedious education or forceful dictation by and from others.

I am an independent soul, or so I force myself to believe – this concept of control, confidence, and security of my being is something I longingly crave, though fail to capture hold of. This, in turn, leads to false hope, senseless aggression, uproar, and an overwhelming dysfunctional coping strategy for the game that is life.

Don't get me wrong, there are certain things I am great at and that I am cut out for, just not in those Young Years, not at *that* place. I had a lot of learning yet to do, not only educational, I had to experience mental learning and understanding.

I must know what it is all about, what this is, what my life is all about; I need to interpret just exactly what my existence is all about.

I remember that day when I left to make my dreaded journey to the school I called *the Freak Show,* where all the complete and utter oddities of life, as I liked to call them, congregated and came together as one; an army of empty ageless souls crying out for need, want, love – sheer desperation from any teacher or guide they could get.

Me? No not me! I never, I don't, I didn't need anyone to get me through this coveted path.

On that particular day on my way to school, it was, thankfully, one of my last to be spent there. I stepped from the safety of my stone-covered hut, i.e. the shelter of the bus stop, and walked onto the moving platform. Strangely, the bus drivers around my hometown conducted their driving skills by keeping the bus travelling between two and four miles per hour. At the same time, the drivers would operate the opening doors, allowing the unknowing or perhaps knowing but impatient, public members to step on and off, all the while. It may have only been a speed between two and four miles per hour, yet it would still be enough to cause one to fall and break an ankle, or an arm, or indeed anything.

I'm a sad catastrophizer, I think such things a lot!

Nevertheless, the only words I had for those bus drivers were 'utterly despicable!' and 'not impressed!' Another sheer pittance of this *life* that had got me down.

I sat down near the back on the left-hand side, next to the window. I could see out my side for once and also out in front of the road ahead. The bus driver was driving at a good speed, twenty-eight to thirty miles per hour, cruising smoothly down each road as if that path was a road to nowhere. I felt at that time I was on my own journey to nowhere. Lost in that very moment of thought, my mind wandered on to the question: *How the hell am I going to get through this? If a simple thing such as a bus and its journey could aggravate me, then what chance do I have?*

The bus was getting closer to my destination. I was wishing that I could drive, though I was too young to drive back then. With hands almost on my head, in slight distress and agitation, I pondered on all the negative thoughts that ran through my mind. They were shrouded by all the dark little clouds low in the sky above, when all of a sudden, the image of a young man appeared in the road ahead. This was a busy road with two lanes to accommodate all traffic; in the mornings it was considered to be a well-used route to drive into Glasgow. I crinkled up my eyebrows with a distinct facial expression as I tried to understand just what the reason could be for this young man to act so uncourteously as he was - standing right in front of the bus!

What in the world was he doing?

Or thinking?

He appeared to be lost. I reckoned that he was around 19 to 20 years of age. Quite tall, perhaps 6 foot in height, he had a slim, medium, athletic-type build. His dark hair was swept to the side with a sleek style of parting. This young man was cute in appearance and nature from what I could make out. I was 14 and to be honest, I thought any young-looking guy was cute - though he, in comparison, seemed sweet. He looked somewhat lost in himself, dazed, a little confused. I, of all people, could definitely understand that! All of this was rushing through my head. I was nervously perspiring, rather restless in my seat, as the bus was fast approaching him when, in a flash, *just like that*, he was *gone*.

The bus, my bus, the one that I was sitting in right there and then, had just run right through him.

The driver, however, was not careless or out of control; he just simply had not seen the young boy. What I did not know at the time was that this was not a person nor a living human being.

This soul, his existence, had passed on. He was dead, a spirit, just a floating wandering soul, alone, confused, tired, trying to find his way into his next chapter, his other realm of life, being, and existence.

It still hurts when I think of it as I can only imagine how he must have died, perhaps in similar circumstances such as those I'd witnessed on that day. I wondered where or who he was now; had he found his resting place, found his home?

All I knew was that I felt the pain, the dark emptiness; I felt him. We were the same though I could not explain why. I too wanted and was looking for my special place, my home, my resting destination. I wanted nothing more than to be happy, content, and significantly serene. I didn't tell a soul what I had witnessed on that day, however, eventually, the day came to tell my mother.

When I did tell her, she had this sad look in her eyes, though joyful at the same time. She knew what I was telling her was something she'd already heard before in my younger years as a sweet, innocent, child.

My mother told me then that I was psychic... whatever that means!

She said I had a special gift, or perhaps even powers!

I thought to myself back then, '*special*'? Witnessing people being mowed down right before my very eyes! Yes, because that must be very '*special*'!

I could not fathom or believe at the time just how my mother could honestly think such a thing. However, what I did not realize at that moment was that this revelation regarding a '*special gift*' was going to be the answer to all of my darkened, heavily invaded, and fear-induced problems. In fact, I was coming ever closer to opening that particular door and discovering it all and all of it.

Did I want to, was the question?

Did I have a choice, was my answer?

CHAPTER TWO

Undying Love for the Unknown

my heart is a child
it doesn't understand endings

K. tolnoe

Emily

I knew as soon as I turned 14 that I had a deep want and longing for a child. Maybe it was not even that I wanted a child, more that I had a need for one.

A very surprising notion at the tender age of 14 years young, to feel that way. However, it felt right, whole, and something that might complete me as a full human being.

Ridiculous! I thought. *How could that be possible - surely it could not?*

I needed to stay focused on navigating my youth and my education; both things that I hate with a passion nowadays.

This never-ending feeling consumed me, this bizarre longing for it.

A child?!

It was the only emotion of love I experienced back then; what else was there?

Yet, somewhere at the back of a deeply drowning and confused mind, there was some sense in there, some belief that my path, at that time, just could not be my only life route. As my mother forever reminded me, '*You only need to look at how I ended up.*'

With those words she would place the strain and hardship she'd endured during my upbringing onto me.

Her fear-filled emotions were now on my shoulders and inserted into my young uninformed and unopinionated mind.

Childlike innocence, no beliefs, unscarred; yet waiting to feel those scars run deep from the external to the internal. I wish now that someone could have prevented it, disarmed it from happening to her and to me, but I couldn't - no one could - especially not my mother.

My father was mainly disinterested in me, though he did not even have the strength to stay for my mother, to help her and to protect her. He just left. He was gone; so were those fragile pieces of my mother's true heart, away with him. I've always truly felt for her sadness, the hurt, and the pain, that I know she suffers. My mother never hid life from me, though sometimes I wish she had!

My first ever encounter with a psychic reading happened when I was 15. The woman came to my grandmother's house to conduct '*readings*' for me, and the other family members. Excited and nervous, I anticipated what was to come. Of course, as fate would have it, out of us all, it was me that was first chosen to head upstairs and into the real-life '*witch's*' den.

The bedroom that the psychic picked to work in was one of my grandmother's spare bedrooms. A dark, little, lilac room at the back of the house, I had always disliked this room in particular and, truth be told, I honestly never knew why, it was just a feeling or vibe I had when I was in that place.

Being an October winter's evening, the mood was dull and wishy-washy. A cool light breeze filled the room, yet no windows were ajar. If I'd used the word *'eerie'* to describe it, I knew that might upset my grandmother's feelings. Although she was a courageous strong lady, she still had real emotions in her.

'Eerie' was most definitely the word for it. Put it this way, I promised myself never to step in or out of that room alone ever again after that day!

This bedroom belonged to my Aunt, my mother's sister. I had always grasped a sense of loneliness from her and that room. She had moved out at a young age and, sadly, years later, she was destined for a young death at the age of 48. She'd suffered from a failing autoimmune condition, which at the point of this event, we knew nothing about.

"Emily?" the psychic gasped. "That's your name, pet?"

"Ahem, what?" I was astonished at this question.

That's crazy! How on earth could this psychic lady know that?!

I was so taken aback that I could as well have been in a time zone completely different from this world I was sitting in right there, right at that moment.

The medium's first name was Pauline, though, for the life of me, I can't remember her surname now. She continued telling me in great detail all of my life's twists and tales, ups and downs, happy and sad times! I couldn't say whether I genuinely believed any of it, though I was intrigued and captivated at the time, excited and apprehensive all at once. However, there was this, still hovering, eerie vibe hanging over us both. Like a thick netting of the most irritating material, it clung to our hair, our skin, and our emotions.

Pauline told me I would have not one but two children by the age of 21, both beautiful daughters.

Daughters? Babies to call my own. I felt such joy.

A strong smile of complete contentment quickly crept over my face. Something was not right though; the eeriness continued to linger in the air. Although I was delighted with the prediction about possible future children, I also felt uneasy and strange, it was almost like I expected bad news next from the psychic lady.

I was aware that everything Pauline was saying was not going to happen to me, or even come close. No matter how much I begged or prayed to whatever God above... No matter how much I wanted it or needed it... No! I just knew it was NOT to be mine.

The medium was oblivious, she carried on with her predictions.

"One day soon, you will start your own business."

Now that felt comfortable for the taking for me, that felt right. I knew inside that YES, that may be possible, that could be it.

My very own business - just imagine? I asked myself mentally, with partial sarcasm.

As I said earlier, there are things I am good at, but money perhaps is not on my list. I don't know! All this was feeling too much on a young untouched heart, I needed it to stop.

I wanted to feel clear in my mind, absolutely crystal clear, with slight hints of purple and lilac, and soft and calming like amethyst, to heal and restore me. I needed that feeling, purposefully wanting to be restored, or even reborn. The thought of this future that lay ahead of me seemed extremely uncertain.

I've never enjoyed feeling uncertain or sitting at ease with it.

I've always wanted to, and have to know, to wholly understand. If there was a video made of my life from start to end - I would take it - hold and cherish just how precious it is, and when the time was right, I'd play it and observe everything, all in the hope that I could make it all okay. They say that when a baby is conceived, the soul still up in heaven chooses its parents - good or bad. Afterwards, the soul picks their life plan and witnesses their entire life ahead of them. It is their choice.

And, supposedly, I had chosen mine...

Did I really choose this though? I don't remember a minute, I don't recall any scenes or moments, but if I did choose this, then I am just going to have to grasp hold of life, this life, and live out the consequences.

Sometimes I think that if I did choose this life, then what other life might I have lived before?

CHAPTER THREE

Night Sweats

*If you can't wake up from the nightmare,
then maybe you are not asleep.*

Unknown

Emily

It happened again!

I was swamped by feelings of being lost and alone, unsure, with nowhere to turn to or go to.

Why was this always happening to me?

Why were these emotions coming to me?

I was 16 and I was just beginning to enjoy life as a mini-adult, with small reminders that I was still a child with loads to learn. I was appreciating everything, along with the thoughts that I had endless amounts of future happiness, yet to discover.

I made my way upstairs to bed, tired from the fast and rupturing hormones that were raging through my body, the energy oozing from my stiff joints, as I slowly crept up the stairs. It felt as though I was trying relentlessly to pull myself up an ice-covered mountain, my body unstable and I was absolutely ready to collapse in a great heap on my bed.

Something stopped me.

Why is it that when you want something so desperately, things or people always get in the way?!

I stopped, startled, as I reawakened within myself, realising with stern horror, what actually lay before me. With one hand on my head, I slouched on my knees in a chair, set perfectly straight in front of the bedroom window. I began to sob and cry.

The room was mostly dark, the only light seeping through from the upstairs hallway ceiling bulb.

At first, there appeared just an outline, though it quickly morphed into a reality.

A girl aged around 9 or 10. Jet black hair, her skin shone pale in the darkness of the room as little tears streamed down her small face. I shrieked for my mother. The feeling within me was as if someone had run full force towards my inner core and stunned me with a blunt object of force. My mouth trembled; words fell silent from my lips. The girl shook with fear, she sobbed more. All the while, I genuinely believed that this person before me had gotten lost from her family or friends, and somehow found her way into my room.

All sorts used to come through my mother's house.

Anything from cats to stray wandering dogs; once a fox came up to the backdoor of the kitchen, no doubt harmlessly in search of food or scraps. Another time, a blackbird came crashing against the window but luckily did not proceed to come through it. The house was even broken into on a couple of occasions by burglars!

It was completely free for all, anyone or anything, to allow themselves in, to join and become part of us.

This safe place that I thought was my home, really was just a house, so it did not surprise me when I found this little girl sitting confused and visibly upset in my bedroom. I was more shocked at WHO she was.

Who was this little girl?

Where did she belong?

My mother strongly held me with a protective nature, long enough to stop my shaking, emotional instability, and the tension that had been vastly forming within my muscles, which were only just keeping my body from falling down.

My mother asked, "What on earth is the matter, Emily?"

I cried more tears now, warming up, slightly burning the fragile skin beneath my eyes, with itchiness on the side.

"What? You don't see her?" I proclaimed.

"Who? What?" my mum responded, worriedly.

"That girl, right there!" I cry, pointing to where the young one sat.

I began describing what I could see when, in an instant, the little girl with the black hair, now apparent that she was indeed more frightened than we, flashed into nothing, disappearing away out of sight.

"Mum? She's gone! What is this? What is going on?" I begged her desperately, awaiting an answer, any kind of explanation.

"It is okay, you are probably just tired Emily, try and get some sleep." To my disappointment that was my mother's response.

I screamed with angst and confusion that in fact, I was NOT tired, even though I, as a matter of fact, was very exponentially exhausted. I tried to explain that this was not the first time I had seen someone or rather something, as I fought with each last depleting spell of energy within me to try and convince my mother of my sighting. I knew deep down she was in whole belief of my discoveries and supported them, all the while worrying continuously about my next encounter.

After that night and most nights since I have awakened to find myself in sheets full of sweat. Cold, prickly, escaping through my skin, seeping through to my bedsheets, even into my mattress. I may have been involved in some form of trauma during my sleep on these nights. Or perhaps living in deep surrounding fear of what lay ahead in this life for me.

Could I not just be normal?

That week for a school art project, I made a gargoyle from molten clay and painted it a standout green colour. They say gargoyles are used to ward off evil and unwanted dark spirits from your life. You can place them anywhere in your home but they're usually placed at the front entrance door, or in any corner of a particular room.

It was most important to me that I felt that warmth of protection all around me, protection being the operative word - it was supposed to protect.

Whether it helps or not, I still do not know.

My night sweats were becoming dreadfully worse; my nightmares were playing a greater game. I suffered from vivid dreams and I truly mean *'suffered'*, as my dreams were like hauntings from another world, another realm brought in to disturb and disrupt my current world, my current realm being here on Earth. I'd go to bed shattered and awaken exasperated and drained, both physically and emotionally.

I did not sleep when I slept.

I lived, I ran, I swam, I flew, I walked, I roamed, I crept.

Or I just simply watched my life happen over and over like a movie - EVERY SINGLE NIGHT!

Chronic nightmares were the medical term for it.

Really? How original! I thought.

It worried me as it was not simply just an adult or adolescent nightmare. For me, it was real life in a dream-like state! I wanted it to stop, to unquestionably end, but that would have been too easy.

Unfortunately for me, it was not on either of my life's 'To Do' and 'Learn' lists.

I was merely resigned to putting up with it, praying that one day I might learn or discover why I was experiencing these dreams.

CHAPTER FOUR

The Girl with the Golden Hair

It is not what you have or who you are or where you are or what you are doing that makes you happy, it is what you think about it.

Dale Carnegie

Pretty was the understatement of the year and content was even more of a distraction, for the well-known and formally accepted, local, general practitioner, Diane Willington.

She had it all - the looks, the designer clothing, the youthful and glowing bouncy hair, the enviable well-kept figure – but, most importantly, she has the true *dreamed-of* life, as well as a loving, wonderful husband, and a beautiful, well-loved, son named Daniel, 5 years old. They appear to be the perfect family; on the outside, they seem to be happy, and they are, except that Diane is not as perfect and happy as many would think.

On the inside, Diane is dying a thousand deaths.

Diane Willington was born in Weymouth, Dorset, England on January 27th, 1947, to her mother, Elizabeth Golding, and father, Gene Golding. Weymouth, a luscious seaside town, situated on a sheltered bay at the mouth of the River

Wey on the English Channel coast. A beautiful mesmerizing town, with breathtaking views, which still to this day attracts thousands of visitors.

Diane's parents were the utmost demanding types, throwing themselves fully into life and more. Sometimes it was just too much to bear, though they believed they were doing nothing wrong. They forced their beliefs and opinions upon their daughter, ensuring her that they were only looking out for her and her future, always.

They needn't have worried as Diane was extremely strong-willed and independently-minded and needed no advice; she had her own ideas and beliefs; no one was allowed to stand in her way.

Throughout Diane's lifetime, she grew ever so fond of Lulworth Cove - Durdle Door. It was for her a special place of retreat; a place of calm and stillness, her best place to be, and she carried that place within her on every step and in every part of her life.

If you stand upon the top of the sensational never-ending height of the Jurassic Coast Cliff, you can look right into Lulworth Cove. The scenery is breathtaking; think of a picture-perfect postcard, absolutely scenic in every sense of the word.

An absolute beauty just standing waiting, at peace with itself before us, before this world.

Diane

My hair would blow gently with the wind; a sweet smell of honey, lavender, and patchouli would ripple past the front of my sun-kissed face, that sweet smell would make me smile, make me feel happy, and allow me to feel truly alive.

It was my most loved fragrance, I wore it everywhere I went; on every occasion.

I loved to spritz it carefully onto my outer clothing, the skin on my neck, and lastly one spritz on either side of my head and onto my golden locks, which shimmered in that pretty summertime Dorset sunset.

CHAPTER FIVE

Lulworth Love

I look at you and see the rest of my life in front of my eyes.

Unknown

The air was fresh, still.

There was a sense of relieving happiness in the surroundings.

My name is Diane Willington; here is my story.

I felt joy and had a skip in my step. I walked casually along with my toes in the slightly warmed sand. The sky above was a light blue with just the odd, bright white and fluffy cloud bobbing past. Laughter could be heard in the near distance, children could be seen for miles as they played on the beach, having picnics at the top of the grass-covered clifftops, enjoying themselves, making the most of their innocence and childhood. Busy creating and living out their future replayed memories with loved ones, and the ones who mattered; the people who cared and were there, though they may not be in the children's impending future moments, or see their most important first played out memories of a lifetime.

I was just 18 years young.

Fun, free.

FREE I was.

I was independent and capable, coping with and at life, no struggles yet. Perhaps the attitude and mentality at that given time aided me through the hard times in life as my guiding light, a line of candles set out along a darkened tunnel.

My parents were often very strict and demanding, the tone in their stern voices was authoritarian, teacher-like. They had the authority that fellow onlooking parents and families envied, they also had a perfect life and did not once ever empathize or feel any sense of compassion for those less fortunate.

Over time, I resented them for that.

It was a part of me that did not exist in my soul or ever develop into my pattern of thinking and behaving. I thought very shallowly of such beliefs. Occasionally, I tried to understand from my mother why behaved in such ways. I, of course, was confronted and reprised with a forceful belt across my right facial cheek with the inner side of my mother's hand. It ached and pain would stem from the area for a couple of hours, the broken and dilated blood vessels on the surface of my skin forming a brightening red pattern. I was embarrassed and I made sure to stay out of the way until at least the colour or reddening purple began to drain away.

I now resented my mother even more; how could she do such a thing?

Could she possibly love me to do that?

Do I love her now, after that?

I had a long time to think. When I sat in my bedroom shut off and out at the very end of the house's long hallway corridor with its high ceilings, Victorian cornices, and large bay draft-riddled single-pane windows. I lay on my single bed and flat on my back. The window was behind my head, upside down. I looked up towards the ceiling, stopping when I could see the sky out of the window.

I got lost in the magic of the moving life that lived above us.

Bringing my thoughts back to my mother and her recent behaviour, I wondered if it had anything to do with my father - he was stern and demanding too. Never could I understand women that put innocent and harmless children through such hurt, upset, and trauma all because they are afraid of *some man.*

Some man they chose to get to know, to marry, to love, to conceive a child with, and then forever suffer greatly at the hands of that possessive man, enduring the verbal and physical torment.

The 'Chained Wives', I call them.

After marriage, the men create this long and strong invisible chain that is forever then attached to the unaware, uninformed wife. They dictate and rule their life from there on! It is pretty sad, but I have witnessed this many times. I have succumbed to this pattern and repetitive way of life. It led me to distrust every man I came across and to never get too close to one as I will not be like the others.

I choose not to become a 'Chained Wife'!

Not now, not ever, never!

Still staring up at the moving sky with a million thoughts of all things said and done running through my head, I tossed myself over onto my stomach and raised my head in both hands.

I remembered the pain in my cheeks, still existent, as I cannot lean too closely onto my face.

Watching, daydreaming, I wish - even pray - though I am not the religious type.

I stood up and opened the single-paned window. It squealed as it retracted outwards. A gust of the beautiful sea air came rushing in, I inhaled then exhaled with relief, along with a little shudder, and gulped in my throat as I held back the fast-filling-up tears in my eyes.

When I looked out, out into the world, I felt like I could be anywhere or anyone.

Something pulled me closer, edging me towards the outside...

I slammed shut the window and grabbed my sandshoes in a fury - I just wanted to get away – right then!

I swung a jacket around my bare shoulders from the back of my wicker chair and proceeded towards the exit of my bedroom and ventured out down the long hallway, the dark but open corridor, down the stairs and through the front door.

I turned the circular latch and mother shouted, "Diane, where are you going?"

"Out," I replied, in a disgraced tone.

I believed at this point mother knew she had done wrong, as surprisingly she let me go. She most likely was worried as she did not know where I was going.

I knew exactly where I was headed - Lulworth Cove.

This place was about to become my place, my new excitement, my home!

The air was fresh, still. There was a sense of relief happening in the surroundings. It took me a while to relax, to get my breath back from all the pent-up anger I held in my lungs, trapped deep within.

I could not let it out or extinguish it, certainly not on anyone in my path, and most definitely not on the one person who deserved it - my mother.

I had to keep walking, one foot in front of the other, hands by my side dangling carelessly, the whites of my sandshoes became grey/black though that did not bother me at all. I began to remember that feeling of joy and half a smile crept from one side of my mouth to the other and changed the look on my face.

It was on that day that I met him.

Tall, slim-built, with an enlightening aura of light swirling all around him, caving him in a protective shield of the brightest colour of white.

I felt this as some sort of power, as an object that I was perhaps supposed to notice.

He shone a smile on me just as the wind subtly rippled past, blowing the outer bottom of my blouse upwards and out, showing off just a hint of my midriff. It was a summer's day, windy but warm. A sleeveless blouse was the perfect attire for the occasion though I was a shy girl; I did not want to give out the wrong impression. I worried too much! My silk blouse was buttoned up in the middle and tied up at the neck in a bow.

We attracted one another with the same white glow expelling from my top, as came from his outer body.

We passed by and at the same time, I shook my head downwards as our bodies were side by side in a parallel form. I could feel him glancing down at me, taking me in, all of me.

I kept walking and felt excited yet disappointed, as nothing came of our passing.

I continued to walk on, head down.

I could hear someone approaching closer, then tapping me gently on my right shoulder, "Excuse me? Sorry, but I think you may have dropped this?"

Shit, I had!

My very first thought was damn it!

Doesn't that just look as if I had deliberately shaken my head just to provoke the attention of the lovely man as he passed by me?

It was my hair clasp. A jade green butterfly with flecks of gold and silver weaved through it. I wore it frequently as I enjoyed wearing pretty things to decorate my youthful golden hair, plus it was a family heirloom that had been passed from generation to generation, and I intended on giving it to my own daughter when she was born and of age.

In a way, this man saved my precious heirloom and returned it to me.

I was embarrassed yet thankful.

When he placed it into the palm of my hand, our skin touched.

I immediately felt a connection, as if a surge of energy had passed within us, bonding us together.

It felt nice, right, I was intrigued as to why this man had crossed my pathway.

I never realized then, just how much I needed an energy like his in my life.

CHAPTER SIX

Reincarnation

You were born to be real, not to be perfect.

Unknown

Emily

I was heading to my new educational establishment where I was taking a photography course. I had discovered a newfound love for this stuff.

Capturing moments, life, people, and nature, all in pictures was a truly fascinating occupation; I was surprisingly excellent at it.

The outside and nature were my ultimate favourite places to capture on camera. I believe the outdoors has a lot to say for itself, even when the air stands stock still when time moves slowly when it seems that the sky does not change one iota for hours gone by.

For my course, I had to buy a professional camera and began practising to pull together a portfolio for upcoming assessments, the prospect of which was exciting and I enjoyed it. As this was a hobby as well as a job for me, it made life that little bit easier.

As I grew older, I liked to think of myself as a bit more middle-class, and I developed this attitude of snobbery. I had more money than I was used to from a student loan I'd taken out, and I decided to become a passenger on trains rather than use the buses.

My look had changed ever so slightly, I began to dress older and wore my hair in a mature and well-kept manner - good enough to be accepted by a member of the royal family, or so I thought. My stance was more upright, along with a perfected gait, as good as any top runway model, as good as a queen.

Elegance came to me as if it were my way of life, how I was supposed to be.

I wore long coats and shoe boots; I was stylish but classy. Feeling this good was surreal, I was living a life that deep down was not and would never be mine, yet I enjoyed it while it lasted.

While on my way to university, I would sit prim and proper on the train from Lenzie station to the city centre of Glasgow, placing my expensive black bag on the seat next to me. Not only did I not wish to get it dirty from the floor beneath, where so many others had walked, I also wished to avoid anyone sitting next to me - simply put... NEAR me!

I have always been antisocial to the extreme, people annoy me! Sometimes I can just look at a person's face, it could be anyone or their mother, and I can instantly take a dislike to them.

Perhaps it's my psychic nature, I've always sensed the good or bad within people. Seriously though, a face, any face, can incite my absolute hate for it.

I secretly and quietly sniggered to myself as I felt relaxed. The journey was a short ten minutes and I occupied myself with a newspaper that lay on the table in front of me. Usually, I would not touch something that had been used by another, however, I was drawn to it, plus I was bored. I needed something to distract me. I flicked through the pages looking at the graphics and designs of the paper.

I passed by a couple of pages and reached page eight before I stopped. Whipping up the bottom corner of the page to turn to the next, I saw a heading saying: *'I Have Experienced Reincarnation'*.

I felt instantly drawn to this, somewhat intrigued, it was as if something within me clicked, twigged, just fell into place. I could not explain my excitement to read this article, so I began, deep in thought, securing my eyes firmly on every word before them. The article was all about people who had gotten in touch and been interviewed on the subject of reincarnation.

They told their stories, explaining how they believed that they had lived before!

Shocked, I was partially in disbelief though I continued. Things that they had experienced in their present lives were all products from their previous past lives; they had such certainty in it that they had been to see people who specialize in this art form. When the reincarnation specialists gave them their past life reports, these people had gone on to research their past lives, finding out that they did once exist, somehow.

One of the believers even documented how they knew that they had family from a previous life, who was still alive here and now on Earth!

Shaking my head, I looked up from the paper and sat for a full minute just thinking how, if at all possible, this could be.

In some distorted way of thinking I felt comfort in this and began to wonder who or what I may have been in a previous life.

Had I been a woman or a man, a child, or even an animal?

All of this deeply intrigued and confused me; I wanted to know more or look further into this! I certainly was not sceptical.

Possibilities are endless and this world has got a lot of answering to do. Nothing is ever plain sailing or will be either.

I've always thought that life is a wondering mystery and that there is more than meets the eye with people, places, life events, and all things that happen. I knew that was why I was drawn to photography, I subconsciously mused if maybe, just maybe, I may capture the unknown, and be able to explain the uncertainties of life.

I felt excited about what was to come next.

CHAPTER SEVEN

Commitment

*Love is the most powerful
and still the most unknown energy in the world.*

Pierre Teilhard de Chardin

Diane

The day when I met Daniel was one of the best days of my life. I had few and far between best days - that was one of them. The instant connection we had was hypnotic, the love we grew for one another was rapid and powered us both.

Daniel was my absolute soulmate, my world, my life.

I often wondered how I'd coped without him, I guess I just plodded along with the hope and assumption that I may find my one true love someday, that he would be all mine and I would be all his, to care, nurture, hold and cherish.

Daniel was a beautiful man; tall, lean, with thick sweeping blonde hair, some strands glimmering in the summer evening's sun. He had a sallow but healthy complexion, all fed by the wonderful sea air that surrounded us. I'd discovered that he lived nearby my parent's house; I never called it 'my house as I never truly felt I belonged there. It was their house that they only allowed me to grow up in, yet I always felt the true burden that I was upon them.

Daniel and I began spending every minute and moment of life we had together and enjoyed each other's company to excess.

The laughter that I never knew could come from within my body, erupted along with great waves and ripples every time he said something.

Usually, it was not what he said, it was how he would say it, that made me giggle away like a little child-free and at peace, happy and content.

I loved every minute, hoping that this and our feelings would last for eternity and that we would never turn to despair or fall out of this deep, intertwining, entrapping cave of love.

With each day that passed we grew closer and closer; almost became one - the same person, divided into two human bodies.

We thought the same way, spoke similarly and shared the same ideas and opinions on life. The more Daniel grew closer to me, his love developed into the type of love you can never forget or move over from. He developed a dislike for my parents at first, though it quickly turned into a sour hatred for my parents. It was their ideas and opinions on life that they shared as a couple that disgusted Daniel and me. Even though my parents were nice enough and treated us fairly and well, you could not distend yourself away from the enticing wall of hate we put up towards them. I was then 20 years old, living life quietly. I was happy too, as Daniel was very much a part of it.

We decided to get married and began making the required plans and preparations to create the perfect day.

A full year had passed and it was now summertime once again, and here it was - our big day.

Our day of love and commitment forever.

The day that we would indeed become one and never let go of what we have, had or hold, for sickness and in health, till death do us part.

The wedding was set to be held at St Mary's Church, Gillingham. I was excited and nervous, though not at the prospect of marrying Daniel, God no! Nervous at the sheer prospect of having all eyes on me and two sets of eyes in particular - my parents.

The church was small yet it was a big wedding, we had many guests and people that had to be there to see us wed, not that they actually meant anything to us, or had our best wishes at heart, they came really just to do their nosey.

If I had it my way, I would have taken Daniel and run away to a place far beyond, where no one could ever find us. I would marry him there, just him and I, alone. Perhaps we would have just one witness.

However, I would want that moment to be entirely unique, exclusive to us, and, most importantly, special in every single way. Moments as precious as that should only be shared with the one true person you love, the one who means the most. To me at that time in my life and that person was him, Daniel my soulmate.

The day had finally arrived!

Beforehand it had felt like waiting an eternity for it to ever occur. Due to all the long and particular preparation that had to go into it all, time took its toll. I was physically shattered, drained, and sick of everyone else's opinions and them butting in on how we should do this or do that.

Excuse me, this is our wedding just me and him, I thought.

I felt a sense of possessiveness strike within me as the deep *'wanting to just escape it all feeling'* once more crept over me. I just wanted Daniel all to myself and myself all to him, no one else, truly no one. They were not there when we met, they did not see our love for each other blossom at the same time, coming from nothing into the best thing that life had to offer. They were not there when we both laughed, we both cried, or when we celebrated and despaired - again at the hands of others. I certainly did not want to share any emotions or moments with them.

My dress was very pretty; ivory and silk.

Both divine and elegant, fit for a princess.

I knew people would look at me walking down that aisle with jealousy and somewhat hatred at how beautiful I knew I would look. Full of myself, I was so far from it, however, I knew I had looks on my side - something that many envied me for.

My hair would be styled and set like a royal queen's crowning glory, finished off with a diamond tiara.

I was confident that I would look the part.

I enjoyed all of it as I've always loved to dress up, making myself the best I could be.

Pretty, not for anyone else though, just for me!

There were the days I'd go out looking all scruffy and rough, with unbrushed hair, not a lick of make-up in sight, and fully dressed from head to toe in dog-walking attire.

I liked those days too; they made me feel like me and brought me back to reality.

Standing outside the church in Gillingham, Dorset, knowing that everyone was inside waiting, anticipating my arrival, and clock-watching to ensure I was not late, even past a minute.

My lungs had seized up inside, deciding they did not want to let me breathe at this moment.

I hyperventilated a little, gasped, and I wondered just for a second if was this what I should be doing.

I did not want it this way so should I have allowed all these other people to get in the way?

I was being ridiculous, I toyed with myself and these thoughts for a matter of seconds before my father pinched my arm in a rather forceful way and said, "Right it is time."

No, I screamed, within.

I started to move as I knew I would feel the instant wrath of my father if I did not begin to walk through those church doors.

The organ player revved up the keys and started to play the typical wedding aisle tune.

Walking in a beat that went along with the organ, we moved slowly down this pathway towards my one true love who was waiting courageously for me at the bottom, smiling.

I swallowed a building amount of nerve-inducing saliva that I allowed to swirl in my mouth for too long, I felt sick.

The tension was coarse and fury filled the air; I did not know why they were there - my parents.

I could feel their deathly stares and presence wading through my back like a hundred daggers, Daniel could feel it too.

Every sound, all words disappeared into a deafening fog that tore away my ability to hear and understand, I could only feel what was going on around me and, believe me, what I could feel was not comforting in the least.

I fantasised for a moment about falling into the puff of my dress, simply closing my eyes shut and enacting my death.

Oh, if that were only possible to escape this surreal situation!

However, what I wanted to do was to scream with all my might and strength, shouting: 'GET OUT! GET OUT YOU HORRORS! THE RUINS OF MY LIFE!'

I could not do it.

"Diane? Diane?"

Just as I felt the overwhelming sense that life was demising me, I was brought back into it; I shook and muttered quietly, "Huh?"

"Diane, do you take this man to be your husband?"

"Yes!" I screamed, in shock and almost desperation.

I sounded as if I needed this more than I wanted it, though it was true I did need it, I needed to be saved.

At this point, after my embarrassing outburst, I heard the crowd chuckle, they found it funny, but they didn't take it seriously.

Neither should have I.

But it was too late, I was too far deep and trained in the whirlpool of paranoia.

My clenched fist, hand towards the man who married us, tightened so much that my nails pierced the skin of my palm, it hurt.

I had done it out of anger, out of pain.

Inner pain.

Although I did not know how intense this pain was yet to become.

Finally, it was over, we were now husband and wife, no longer a Willington, I was now a Murrison.

Diane Murrison.

CHAPTER EIGHT

The Shortest Day After the Longest Night Before

You can't sell dreams to someone who has walked through nightmares?

Unknown

Diane Murrison

It was a nice day, our wedding day, followed by a nice afternoon, even a nice night, '*nice*' being the operative word.

I wished it could have been different, with just the two of us there.

That's how it should have been.

Nevertheless, it was a nice day, once I'd overcome the initial fear and worry of what everyone else might be thinking and, of course, saying about me.

Turned out they had only words of kindness and love to share and send our way, which I appreciated, and then felt a little more relaxed when I discovered this.

It was extremely hard being in my mind - this mind of mental torment, this anguish - all of the time. I hid it, and I hid it well. I tried. Half of me was happy and full of joy, while the other half of me was screaming out, trying to run through thick black smog with no way out, no opening, no saving myself.

It was the 'no zone' where no one, nothing, not even me, could get in or out, which is a lie I always got through and I ended up in.

Always I wound up stuck and losing sight of how to get out.

Daniel had come up behind me, embracing me in his long, sturdy arms, just below my neck. He always had such a calming warmth exhaled from his body, and his smell, oh my God, his smell - it was the nicest thing! Natural, with a hint of self-applied body fragrance, plus of course, a male essence. His smell would linger around for hours after his soft skin caressed mine.

It gave me comfort, I guess I had never experienced such comfort before.

I had, but not from someone whom I truly loved – Daniel.

He asked what was wrong, he could always tell even if he hadn't been looking directly at me for ages, he would just know that something was wrong.

I joked he had a sixth sense and we would laugh forever about this.

Was it my short silence?

My duller tone of voice?

My non-enthusiasm, which I occasionally battled with in life?

None of these; he just knew.

He just knew me.

I smiled, although he could not see.

I smiled because I just told myself to: *Get a grip and don't dare let him know anything is wrong, because it is not fair, it is me that is wrong, my person, my make-up.*

However, I did not want to burden him with this, so my smile grabbed me and woke me to a better shape of me, a happier me, the me that lied when he queried as to what was wrong, I'd reply, "I am fine darling, absolutely fine, why do you ask?" I'd send him a question back as if to make him feel uneasy for asking it in the first place.

"Oh nothing, was just checking to you are all right. I love you, Diane," he would softly retort back at me.

His words lifted me and made me realise what was important once again.

We sat together, rummaging through some of the wedding gifts that we'd received. People had been very generous and giving; we did not need this number of gifts, or indeed any of these kinds of things. Plus, I had my own taste and twist on everything.

I bundled some of the items together, packs of hi-ball glasses, champagne flutes, vases, and even a new toaster. I made my way along to our kitchen; it was cosy though big enough. I enjoyed my space but this space was quiet. I placed everything down on top of the nearest dumping area I could find and I sighed with exhaustion and despair; to be completely frank, I could not be bothered in the slightest to deal with all this right now.

I was tired mentally; I just wanted to stand and stare which I did while looking out of my kitchen window that sat above the sink area. The window was large and I adored the scenic view with the grass-covered field, the trees, and the blue sky - my favourite.

Suddenly I heard rummaging and a smash coming from the sitting room where Daniel was.

Rushing in, I found him with a broken teapot in his hands, "It slipped, I'm sorry."

I could not care less - it was a china teapot, handed down as a gift. It could go in the bin as far as I was concerned, yet I still felt annoyed as I quietly thought to myself, *Why can they never get it right? Men, are they really just that simple? Women always have to clean and tidy up behind them.*

These thoughts came with a bitter disturbance and attitude that I did not like.

I scurried away, up the stairs to lay down on our now marital bed and closed my eyes.

For that one time, that moment, I wished that all the thoughts would just go away and that it would all feel okay again!

Then it occurred to me that my poor loving husband was sitting all alone downstairs with the broken teapot, trying to make the best out of a bad situation, trying to help. This was something this man did, something that my man did - Daniel helped me in more ways than one.

I sat myself up slowly and in sheer depression, I sighed, it was more like a silent scream, I felt so angry and irritable though I must carry on.

I got up and made my way downstairs and there he was, looking all sheepish and worried, and there was me, the crazy mental case that couldn't harm a fly but could do more damage with my thoughts and words with no time to think… However, with always plenty of time to regret.

Just at that moment, something occurred to me and I did not feel guilty, I felt ready for a war! It was a war I wanted to start that may only consist of a few people and one that may leave me in the type of place I never thought I would see.

He looked at me, though this time with disappointment in the glare of his eyes.

It made my stomach turn or jump, I could not fully explain it, although I had this sense of eternity becoming vastly cut short - with him.

I made my way into the kitchen and gathered up in one hand a wine glass and the bottle of Rioja from the cupboard, I clinked them both onto the wooden dining table and sat on the chair. Bearing in mind it was only 2 o'clock in the afternoon, so perhaps a little early to be opening a bottle of wine.

I needed it though, or something else, to take the edge off my nerves and frustration of pent-up anger.

Daniel paced in, "Do you really think that is a good idea, Diane?"

"Well, what is?" I replied, in a demeaning manner.

This was the man I loved with all my heart and soul, every inch and crevice of my body, and my emotions swamped him.

I was in love with him, yet, there I was, sitting and staring into this glass of red wine, contemplating, *Where do we go from here?*

I took a sip of my drink.

Is this really truly what I need or want? I asked myself.

A purpose was what I wanted, a logical meaning for life - I wanted to be wanted, and feel alive, encompassed in someone else's love and admiration of ME.

The 12% alcohol content of my Rioja wine had quickly turned day into night and before I knew it, I was sitting alone in the dark as Daniel had left me, departing upstairs to bed for the night.

He had had enough.

I was on my own, surrounded by self-pity with only my bottle of red, now empty, for company. It was not fulfilling at all, I only felt worse, trapped, and in panic mode with a gnawing, dulling sense of emotion that engulfed my withered head.

My body was overflowing, drowning me in drunkenness, the type of feeling all drug addicts must get when they first inject - that feeling of reality slipping and fading away, day-to-day life and everything within it, dissipating into the mystical wilderness above.

It was time for bed, time to rest, to go to sleep and to hope that all would be fine in the morning.

CHAPTER NINE

Attraction

*The fantasist denies reality to himself,
a liar does so only to others.*

Friedrick Nietzsche

Emily

I was now in my prime at the grand age of 21, living it up, I would go out everywhere and anywhere I could, with whomever I could. I was now midway through my photography degree at Glasgow University in the West End of the well-known town. It was very posh down there, prim and proper.

Sometimes I felt as if I did not fit in, that I was just not one of them.

How could I possibly be? I was just an ordinary girl from a small lesser-known area out of Glasgow city. The suburbs, the rural land, that's where I was at home. From somewhere I plucked up the courage I desperately craved and needed to succeed in this short phase of my life, which at the time felt as though it was going to trickle on forever, like a never-ending sludge of a dark, muddy river, continuously dampened with further rain, storms pouring down, prolonging its existence even further.

Each day in my life was a long battle with myself and others.

You see, I hated other people so much. I mean I liked and still like the very few, it's just the majority who never make or made the cut, forever locked up in the box in my head marked, '*Detest*'.

I've always found most people to be very different from myself, just slightly strange.

People with attitudes, disloyal folk, two-faced friends, and jobsworths.

To be honest, I hate them all, and still do, though I know that feeling this way is bad and wrong, I feel that they have wronged me, coming into my life and crossing my pathway with that ignorance and distasteful attitude.

I would tell my mother these thoughts I had about people and she'd say, "It's because you are not for this world, for this life. You are different - this is Hell and you are an Angel who has been put into the wrong realm."

I thought it was funny back then, however, I now believe it to be very true. I know that there is something far better beyond all of this; I just don't know when I will get to go there and see it.

I had chosen photography as I wanted to see the world for what it was - places, people, and things. I wanted to see it in full colour and in black and white.

Photography to me is art, a powerful and underestimated art, the things you can capture in a photo speak a thousand words and descriptions.

When I felt sad I would photograph the sky looking grey and cloudy and I'd print the photo and fall into it, I'd lie with it and make up a whole story in my head about that photo and its surroundings. It would make me feel safe in myself and keep me from harm; it would accept me and my feelings, as it felt so deep, dark and low in itself.

Other days would be good and happy; I would perhaps go out and capture something of a fun, loving state, such as a deer in the field next to where I lived. I noticed the deer being so very quiet and still yet weary and fearful; always on the watch out for harm, targets and trickery. They made me feel better, they made the sun light up in the sky as they wandered mercilessly through the golden haze of the grassy field.

I would want nothing more than to throw a checked blanket on that grass and lay down looking up above or ahead.

Anywhere, just not where I was.

A fantasist, I longed for a different world to be in, filled with different people and where things were good and free, where I could feel truly safe at long last. Four days a week I attended my photography course and it's fair to say I was barely there, for as much as I loved it, I hated it equally. I didn't like being told what to do, nor did I do as I was told. We spent a lot of our precious exam nearing days in pubs and lunching out as if we owned the riches of the day. The student loan was pretty damn good and I made sure to enjoy myself while I still could.

I knew the day would come when I may be tied up in some other opportunity that I would liken to a prison – well, that is what life is, isn't it - a prison?

All the inhabitants on the merry-go-round of work, in order

to live their lives. Never-ending, until it does end one day and where we, once again, have no control.

I wanted to live so bad, I wanted to go and be free, I wanted to know everything there was to know.

I began having dreams again. Night sweats, terrible night sweats! Why wouldn't they stop?

I believed that something or someone was trying to contact me, or perhaps send me a message. I felt pressure to find out just what that message might be.

Whom could it be?

And why?

After a long day and an afternoon of drinking, I headed back home and went straight to bed. I needed to dream again, get away from here for the night. I had to find out what these dreams meant. My eyes relaxed shut and my head was slightly spinning when I turned to the left as I lay on my back.

It was time to drift off and away, headed to this other world that I had been dreaming in.

Time to revisit and time to discover what it was all about.

CHAPTER TEN

The Dream

With dreams so vivid, I begin to wonder if, in fact, they are not dreams, but forgotten memories.

Unknown

Emily

I awoke mid-morning feeling rather unrefreshed. I'd had the night sweats again, either from all the cheap spirits I had consumed during lunchtime of the previous day, or it may have been the fact that I had the recurring dream again.

I felt uneasy when I thought about the dream, though I was unaware of any reason for that - perhaps the dream was really part of a bigger nightmare.

As I lay flat on my back, staring at the artexed ceiling, my bed felt warm and cosy; I was snuggled up and nearly smothered by the enormity of the thick winter duvet on my king size bed.

I felt the cold outside of the covers as it engulfed the room, however, I stayed deep within them, avoiding exposure of any part of my skin to the sharp morning breeze.

I began to replay the dream in my head, desperately trying to remember the little parts or anything at all, and in as much detail as I was able. Although I knew it was just a dream, something resonated inside of me like a flashing or pulsating light giving off warning signals that caused me to anxiously want to focus on as much of it as I could.

I remembered the crashing sea rushing in furiously up against a tall, rocky hill, the side of which was mud covered, or most likely a mixture of sand, earth dirt, and seawater.

I even remembered the sound of the waves as they crashed in and that unbalanced feeling it gave my body whilst being a witness to it.

It frightened me and left me nervous, especially as I did not know what to expect or what might occur from the sea waves being as angry as I had seen them.

I looked and watched people standing along the side of the sea and as the water rose up into a large cavernous wave, it came swirling up and over those innocent bystanders, taking them, as if the sea gods were having a very bad day and wanted to discharge every ounce of aggression they could, despite what damage it might do. Standing very slightly back although not far enough to be in the distance, I was just far enough not to be harmed by the demon-like possessed waves.

I watched in horror and amazement all at the same time.

This could be the end for me, just as it was certainly the end for those innocent bystanders, who had been standing there on the coast on that day in my dream.

I thought back to how angry the sea had been and I questioned if the people that succumbed to it were not so innocent after all, maybe they were bad or had been bad in the past.

Perhaps it was their karma catching up with them.

Maybe they had deserved it and maybe it was the sea gods' revenge because the waves never took me. They wanted me to watch for some reason, or did they?

I felt empowered to know and destined to find out.

As the dream continued, the waves began to settle and, in all strangeness, I made it through that devastation to reach the next part of my journey. I had begun to walk along a golden sand-covered beach. I felt the heat beneath my toes, the slight crunch and jagging of prickly seaweed and stony rocks. I heard laughter and joy, as I felt a sense of being drawn to up above, on the sand dune rock hill.

As I said before, it was a mixture of all types of material and it was dazzling, very bright indeed. Yellow, orange to be precise, though I could see grass just peering ever so slightly over the edge at the very top.

I felt strange again, uneasy like I wanted to look and to see so badly, yet a magnetic force appeared to be pulling me away from setting my sights up there. I turned my head around and back down to the walkway in front, still on the sandy coastline, walking freely and in the startling sunshine.

I continued to walk.

In fact, it felt as if I had travelled miles in just one moment, then isn't that the craziness of dreams - dreams are a subconscious belief we carry in our minds.

Everyone dreams - I truly believe this - yet the fact is not everyone remembers their night full of being whisked off into some other realm or world.

Some people have good, nice, happy dreams, while others have nightmares filled with terror and scares, confusion and worry, and others dream of the future.

I've had many dreams over the years where I actually dreamt the future; it was bizarre, of course, and at the time I did not know that what I was waking up from was actually a disturbing insight into the next day or two world's events.

I would dream certain things and not think too much about them or dwell upon them, then I'd discover my exact dream play out on the news just a day or so after.

That would upset me as I felt I could have or should have done or said something to stop it from happening. Of course, it was almost certainly always devastation and tragedies I received in glimpses and insights. It was horrible.

Sometimes though, I would have dreams that I knew were just for the good of me.

I also had another recurring dream much less frightening than one of the crashing sea waves coming at me and everyone else within it. This particular recurring dream was a bit nicer that that one. Yes, it was warming and lovely to see and experience, however, occasionally it left me full of both doubt and wonder.

I was in this dark small kitchen getting ready to go out enclothed in a navy waterproof raincoat. I must have been a lot older as I felt around the thirties mark and this boy appeared - small, blonde hair, around six years old.

I bent down to him, he had the sweetest and most innocent face I had seen on a young child, and he wrapped his little arms around me, holding on tight, as he whispered in my ear, "*Mummy, you are the best mummy ever, and I am so glad you are mine; I will look after you, you will be okay, just don't leave.*"

I replied, "*Of course, I love you too and I will always love you.*"

It was strange as it felt as if the boy was not coming with me, he was left behind, but if that was the case who was watching him? As usual, my motherly instinct kicked in at that point, even though I did not have children yet.

It was a very maternal feeling and I shrugged, assuring myself that it was only a dream.

As I took myself back to what happened after I or this woman left the little child behind, I remembered she then proceeded to walk out of the house. We ended up in a graveyard. She was wandering around slowly, with yellow flowers in her hands, I can now only describe her in the second or third person tense, as I no longer believe that I was the woman in this dream.

I believe I was watching someone else through my eyes, however, this somehow had a connection to me.

As this woman walked along on each of the graveyard pathways, I recalled her having light blonde hair and a red waterproof raincoat, she was slim build and appeared elegant as she had grace in her gait. She appeared to be looking for something, back and forth she would go, until eventually her body movements came to a halt and she gazed for a couple of seconds before lowering herself down toward a particular headstone, where she then laid down the yellow flowers.

At this point I remember looking all around me and taking in my surroundings, I could see that the graveyard I was in had a very high wall all around the perimeter, perhaps safeguarding it and protecting it from unwanted intruders. The wall was very white in colour and looked recently new, there was an opening at the mid-point that looked to me like the entry and exit. The grass and halfway trees looked beautiful and well nurtured, it was a very calming, quaint place to be.

Weirdly, I enjoyed my time there.

All at once, it would be over and I'd wake up wondering, curious, and dumbfounded as to what I'd just experienced.

This was not just a dream, it was extremely vivid and surreal, it pretty much made up the whole content of my sleep that night.

CHAPTER ELEVEN

Surprises

You should not have to rip yourself into pieces to keep others whole.

Ritu Sharan

Diane

Two years had passed since our wedding; I now had my degree in medicine and I was keen to get on with becoming a doctor.

This had always been my dream – finally, it was coming true.

I was feeling pleased with myself and although I was a little scared as to what I may experience in this line of work, I had an open and upbeat attitude towards it. On the other hand, Daniel, who was an engineer, was keeping himself busy in that role. Together we were building an exuberant life, full of everything we'd ever wanted. Things were going great and at last, we were happy.

From time to time we would get the odd person asking us, "So, what about children now?"

It never failed to shock and disgust me that people would ask this kind of question outright - how dare they, it's none of their business!

I would reply, "Of course, soon. We both would love a child."

Sick of people's ignorance and interference, I found it extremely rude, however, they did not, they had absolutely no filter, and words would just seep through like rainwater would come through the cracks of an old sash window.

Yet, I had to be kind and polite and answer them with absolute grace, just as I'd been doing my whole life, giving them no cause to talk about me. I never wanted them to talk about me, they were complete gossip.

Every day I would get up and go through the exact same routine before heading to work at the doctors' surgery in Dorset, just a couple of streets away from my house. I could walk to work; it was good I suppose. At 6.30 am, I'd go into the bathroom clean my teeth and face, and so on. Next, I'd proceed to make breakfast, if I could face it. Afterwards, I'd get myself dressed in smart attire such as a nice pencil skirt or suit and comfortable low-court heels. The time would now be 7.30 am as I'd collect the few things I'd need for the day and I'd pack my bags, personal and my doctor's case. Once ready I'd leave the house and begin walking to work, arriving at 7.50 am, ready for my first patient of the day at 8 am.

I DID THIS EVERY DAY – now, I don't know how I did it.

Dull and monotonous - the job, the life, the everything - well, what else?

Yes, nothing else.

There was nothing else.

I felt completely miserable, I did not know why.

Perhaps it was all the patients coming into the surgery day in, day out, moaning, complaining, muttering - the depressed ones - because they can't speak, they have absolutely zero confidence in themselves. I felt for them I really did, as at some point, it gets to us all.

Depression is a real thing, in fact, it's a major thing, something people like to ignore, pretend that it is not real, that it doesn't exist, that it doesn't happen to them. However, it does, it is real and sad, extremely sad, but God do I hate the *muttering*, just speak, just say how you feel, and speak loud for help, for goodness sake.

Arrr...! I just want to scream at them, scream at everyone! This is useless, cannot go on like this, I am a professional, and I need to be more caring and understanding.

I hated my patients.

I thought I was not cut out for this job, this GP malarkey. Infused as it was with busy and fussy parents who wanted the best.

Well, guess what, sometimes the best doesn't tend to be the best, it tends to be the worst and, in turn, I am suffering.

Should have just let myself make my own mind up as an adult about what adults are supposed to do. A person is not born to parents, only to be told what to do with their whole life, how ridiculous. Stupid me, doing what I was told. So, I'd go from work and back home, to work and back home, and so on.

Pathetic, useless, unreal, cannot go on.

Yet again the questions, 'Oh married now, children yet?' blah

blah blah. I really felt unsure about it all and wondered if children were meant for me.

I partially liked them.

If I saw a stranger's children, depending on the parents, I would judge that child a hundred per cent on them. If I didn't like the look of the parents, I would not be keen on their children, it was an instant turn-off. Tragic, I know, but then I was tragic, horrible.

The more I pondered on the subject of being a parent, I thought it was what I wanted.

I planned to take some time off to myself. Stupidly I believed that it was wholeheartedly where all mothers went wrong - believing the unbelievable, the unreality - because reality is so very different. Hmm... a short holiday away from my work life and hectic schedule that I currently hated, eight months of carrying a baby, then a month to one's self, then eight to nine months of maternity leave. Bliss, just bliss.

Exactly what I needed - a complete holiday - no doubt about it and then, what everyone always says, 'a beautiful little baby' – at the end of it.

Finally, I was coming around to the idea, beginning to feel slight excitement, slight joy. I thought about the unknown and how it could be exciting and deeply intriguing. I always longed for the unknown, somehow it made me feel at one with myself and that there is more to this life.

One night I arrived home after a usual dreary day at work. I began to find my husband tangible, well at least I had to know if he was the one I aimed to begin a family with. I sat him down to eat the dinner that I'd prepared earlier and went on to cook fully. I poured some white wine and dished up the meal.

When he was a quarter of the way through, I blurted, "I think we should have a baby."

Daniel was astonished.

Not because he didn't want or desire children, he did; he was broodier than I was. He wanted little babies more than any man I had known. I just always put the idea off and away, so now that I was offering up the idea, he reacted as extremely shocked, though, the more he thought about it, the more he loved the idea.

He looked at me and said, intensely, "Yes, of course."

My husband went on to say that I knew that was all he had ever wanted and so on. He was the extremely soppy type, loving, but sometimes a tad too much. Possibly he was of this nature because at times he lived with a cold-hearted bitch who demanded too much, sometimes wanted love, sometimes wanted to fight, sometimes wanted to be happy, and sometimes wanted to be sad.

It was a complete up-and-down rollercoaster, merry-go-round, fucking nightmare.

Why wouldn't it be?

It was me, his wife, the flawless Diane.

The perfect woman - on the outside and to everyone. On the inside, a complete lunatic, with crazy extreme oddities to go along with it.

After dinner, Daniel and I sat discussing it all evening; the baby.

I should mention that it was mainly Daniel that had led the discussion about it. Ideas for names, what the baby may be, its colour of hair, and how it would look like. I felt uneasy, why I honestly did not know, I wished I didn't but I did; I should have known but was yet to figure it all out.

With every ounce of his excitement came my every ounce of despair, frustration, and disbelief.

Still, I had to remain straight-faced, calm, a 'yes' woman, as this is what I'd decided that I wanted right now, this was the time, I hoped, I really hoped.

He asked, "When should we start trying for the baby?"

I looked at him blankly in response. *Ha! Oh yes, shit, it's real now*, I thought.

Then, I replied, "We need to start now, it's a new life, a big change."

He was happy.

I hoped it would happen, but at the same time, I hoped it would not.

Heads can be a mess at times like these. So, gone were any forms of protection and it was all gung-ho from that moment on. Again, the thought of the unknown and whether or not it may happen, and when it may happen, all intrigued me, spurring me on, even with the slither of worry that lay at the back of my mind - where I needed it to stay.

This was all Daniel had ever wanted and it was what I planned to give him. The family life, the precious first child, then more children, the security, the home life.

What I wanted was peace and quiet, calm, and routine but in the midst of that, I just wanted a holiday. I was not ready for a complete life change.

I was not ready for this.

CHAPTER TWELVE

Beginnings and Endings

Faith is the bird that feels light and sings when the dawn is still dark.

Rabindranath Tagore

Diane

I sat, I waited, I watched and I anticipated whether it would be two lines or one. In a food shop customer toilet cubicle. My heart was beating worryingly fast and my palms sweated. I knew I didn't want this but I could not stop thinking of the hurt Daniel if he was let down again, and again.

It was negative, the pregnancy test.

It was not to be, at least for now. I knew it would happen at some point or other, but it was not right now. That was fine by me. I felt too uptight, over worked, over stressed and drained by physical life itself to even consider or worry about bringing new life into this - this shit hole with shit faced people.

One evening the week before, I'd told Daniel that I thought everyone in the world was a cunt and I would tell them all that they were a cunt to their faces! He'd been genuinely disgusted.

Why was I like this, why did I feel this severe, I wanted the world to stop, I wanted it to pause, everything and everyone.

It's too fast, I thought, you reach a certain age and it goes past like a train on speed. I want to dance, I want to run, I want to just scream, to sweat tears of joy and laughter, not despair and exhaustion.

But it was to be the latter.

How was I to go back and tell him? What was I to say?

Just awful again, another disappointment too and for us, for our beautiful little world, for our happiness. I knocked my fist against my head once, then again and again, until I just grimaced inside. Then I froze until I stopped completely still within this sense of calm and quiet, unknown yet undisturbed, as I enjoyed the peace of that moment of silence, just one moment that I revelled in.

Emily

My photography career was well and truly taking off as jobs were rolling in.

However, I still felt the lingering uncertainty and everlasting curiosity feeling or vibe that controlled my thought processes, clouding my wants, ideas and aspirations.

It was the thought of what was missing from my life - what was missing I asked.

Over and over. It's like I knew this was all right and I knew what I needed to do, but why did I have this particular and unrelenting tapping sound, somewhere at the back of my never-ending mind process?

It's hard to describe, hard to contemplate, just that feeling of knowing, wanting to know and finding out once and for all.

Over the years some people would question things as they tried to help me to figure out my life and to discover perhaps why I was the way I was.

At times, for the majority of the goddamn days of my life, I was a good, gentle, normal woman.

People thought, however, that they could just wade in, pointing out certain factors that they had potentially seen as important, or an obvious threat to my life. They would tell me that was partially the reason why two-thirds of me included a part of me that was empty and a part of me that was unknown and not right, as yet undiscovered.

"So tell me about your dad, Emily?" one of them would ask me.

"Ehhh , emmm, hmm… Well, I don't know him, never have, don't know anything about him, so…" I'd reply.

"Ahh right, so do you ever think that has possibly had an impact on you growing up? Have you ever wondered about your dad? Perhaps you feel different because you never knew him?" the inquirer would surmise.

Invisible question mark upon question mark.

The other would sit there awaiting my answer while watching as my eyes rolled and flickered.

Meanwhile, I would hear my brain as it ticked away, thought, felt frustrated and then contemplated the question, understanding all in one little breath, maybe two.

Finally, my answer, after all, would be, "No. How can you miss something you have never known?"

It is strange after all; I did at times while growing up in this wonderful world, wonder what may it be like to have a dad.

A dad, a real dad, what must that be like, how must that feel, how must life play out if you have a mum and a dad?

My friends' dads growing up never usually seemed all that. They had appeared glum, quiet, uninterested, and somewhat ever so small. They looked suspiciously like that look when you're living a double life when you're not the man everyone thinks you are, when you are hiding things from your own family, your children, your wife.

I'd look straight into their eyes as deep as I could go without being too nervily obvious. They would look back at me with a quick, 'hmm... oh shit', with a flicker and a twitch.

It was like they knew that I know; I know these things.

I honestly do not know how, I just do; I just know.

However, then I thought to myself, God what was it though that they have done or are doing? Now I really wanted to know after all! It's mad. Are they cheating? Frauds? Double-life leaders also come under the bracket of cheats and paedophiles.

I did, believe it or not, come across this once; a disgusting excuse for a man, who was meant to be or supposed to be *holier than thou*, a man who was a devout Catholic, who had enforced his religion and beliefs upon his whole family, his wife, his eldest daughter, who happened to be the same age as me at the time, and his younger daughter who was only a few years younger than us. His eldest daughter and I were friends.

Sometimes I'd think of that man and ask myself, *why did God give him daughters? If there is a God?*

I supposed that with people such as him, it would have been just the same if he'd fathered sons.

We would go and play up at their house at the weekends, we would have been around 8 or 9 years old at the time. The first time I ever entered their house, something struck me, whether it was the colouring of their decorations and furnishings – everything, and I mean everything, was a dirty, discoloured, washed-out shade of brown, that had lightened in some parts to a shade of beige. It made me feel almost sick. The house was bare and didn't have much in the way of furniture, they had rags for curtains draped down over the windows which were always covered. The curtains were always drawn as if there had been a death daily. In the living room, there was a couch that was old and tattered, with multiple crosses and crucifixes around the place. The lightbulbs were all bare and exposed in each room, without lampshades to dampen down the light that expelled from them, not that there was much. This made me feel uneasy, I had never seen this form of lighting before in my younger years, I felt it strange not to have lampshades. I felt it strange for them to have this type of life and living arrangement. Something wasn't right. I succumbed to this wave of exclusive darkness, a darkness I had never experienced before, the type of darkness that has no light, the type of darkness that ends it all. It suffocated me, it engulfed my whole being, my breath, my life. Smoke filled the room, I couldn't see the ceiling for the layered ring of smoke pooling all of the above and sweeping through every crack and crevice, softly landing on the ragged curtains, seeping into the couch, it was anywhere and everywhere but the outside, leaving nowhere to escape from it, nowhere to be free, nowhere to go, trapped forever until someone let it free.

The first time I saw him, we had locked eyes, except when he locked eyes with me he grabbed mine as if with both of his hands and every might in his small body. His dark brown eyes strangled my eyes, held them tight and would not let go. It seemed as if minutes had passed before finally the release came, finally I was let go. My head shuffled back and I felt I had to realign myself, felt I had to get some strength back.

"This is my dad," my friend said, proudly. My young innocent friend who thought he was her world.

"Oh hi," I greeted, aghast, the expression on my face never changing.

I think my friend breathed a sigh of relief almost and felt good to get that over with.

I looked deeper towards him and then back at my friend and I asked her, " Can we go play now?"

That room needed to be free of us, that room was just for him and his eyes, and his cigarettes. He watched intensely, his stare boring right through our backs, as we walked down the dark smoky corridor and turned left into my friend's bedroom.

Inside, two beds, one for her and one for her sister, I supposed. Toys lay scattered around the floor, they look worn and dusty, as if they were just there for some kind of decoration from the house of horrors.

But, the true horror was yet to come.

In the corner of the room stood a table and over the table hung a long, ivory silk dress with some netting fabric attached; a wedding dress.

I said, "What's that?" in complete excitement.

I thought, Wow! An actual real wedding dress - How amazing!

Being a typical girly girl, I wanted to grab it, twirl around with it in one hand and let gravity and the little air around us swish the dress from one side, then 180 degrees to the other.

My friend explained that it was not a wedding dress and that I was silly for thinking so. She told me it was her communion dress and explained in our following conversation that it all means to marry God. I thought that was fair enough as I didn't know much about it.

I asked, "Why is it out here, lying on a table, should it not be somewhere safe?"

Even at the young age of 8/9, I was old enough to know an expensive garment such as that shouldn't just be left lying around as it might get dirty or even damaged. That's when she struck me with the impossible comment that still haunts me to this very day.

"My dad likes me to put it on each day and to have my communion with him, so I can be married to my dad."

At the time I did not exactly see what was wrong with this, as I didn't know or understand their religion. I thought that this very well may be the case for Catholicism, but also due to not having had a dad myself, I did not quite comprehend that marrying your dad could even be a thing.

How very wrong I was and how very strange events were about to turn...

CHAPTER THIRTEEN

The Mad, the Ugly and the Evil

Sooner or later, everyone sits down to a banquet of consequences.

Robert Louis Stevenson

Emily

I never told anyone what I had found out about my friend and her dad, I thought I did not fully know the extent of what it was she had told me.

Plus, what if she had just made it all up?

It could have been a make-believe, pretend story, so at the age of 8/9 I wasn't exactly going to run and inform the whole neighbourhood of the strange events at number 26. My friend's mum always struck me as strange too. Very timid lady, plump, but almost frail within herself. A delicate ornament that could crack at any second if knocked over, that was her mum. The mum who married her dad, the dad that I utterly could not get over, with his extremely hostile, darkened vibe, which emanated from him with his every breath. It was as if he was dead, merely existing, but existing all the same in a grave form.

I wondered why had her mother married such a man?!

I assumed that there had been happiness to some degree within their marriage, mainly at the beginning when they first met, but more than likely it had now fizzled out as they had grown older and had children, or perhaps because she found out just what kind of a man he was.

Why did she stay?

Why didn't she scoop her precious babies up, no matter how old or grown she thought they were at that time - just scoop them up and take them, away to anywhere - anywhere that was away from him.

Being the age I am now, I understand what it must be like to go through such a thing and how dreadfully hard it would be to walk away, to leave everything you have built, all the things you own, memories, and treasures, all to walk, to run away and escape the evil you have enveloped yourself and your family in.

It must have been hard - I do not know.

But why let that kind of thing going on right under your nose?

From what I had gathered and seen, I don't recall her working, as I remember she was made to stay at home, not as a homemaker or a housewife, nor even as a mother or a cook, but as a prisoner.

A prisoner in her own home.

He was a control freak, a worrisome, endless threat, type of man. He degraded her and controlled her every thought, word and movement. I found this all out for certain many years later when my mum bumped into her in a shop that she had found herself working in, it was good to see her out of the house and in a job. It was good to see her safe and well.

We were happy for her that she had a happy ending with her children.

It was the end of summer 2001, and the last of us children were out playing in the street as usual, the sky was a nice hue of warm orange with purple flecks, as the sun was trying to set over a dusky Glasgow. I hadn't seen my friend for a while and thought she had been away to stay with family. Suddenly, a van pulled up at number 26 and some men got out, then they proceeded into the home where my friend lived.

I heard in an almighty roar, "Get in right now!!" It was my mum shouting, she sounded both worried and angry all at once.

Of course, I was intrigued and wanted to stay and watch, however, my mum kept repeating, "I don't want you to see this. I don't want you to watch this."

My mum obviously knew something I didn't, she knew who the men from the van were and predicted what was yet to occur. A few minutes passed and I peeped out from my upstairs window as I could get a good direct view from there to my friend's house, and there it was. Her dad was being guided by these men into the van, he looked different, he looked grey and dishevelled, he appeared calm and walked slowly, although the men were eager to get him into the van that was parked out front.

Then I said, "Mum what is he wearing? What is that white jacket he has on?"

My mum then had the unfortunate job of explaining to me what a '*white jacket*' meant, what someone's arms being tied up around the jacket meant.

It was a straitjacket.

Astounded, I listened closely as my mum described what sort of people got taken away in straitjackets.

Nowadays, I would imagine that he'd be among one of the last people to be taken away in a straitjacket. Due to human rights these days, it's not something that the mental health team would enact upon a person, no matter how bad they are, or what wrong they have done.

I still do not know to this day the exact reason as to why he was taken away in that straitjacket, nor where he was taken to, although I eagerly presume a mental facility, where he would no longer be of harm to himself, or anyone else, such as his daughters for that matter, and most definitely, his long-suffering wife. I do know she unfortunately and unfairly suffered at the hands of him on many occasions. It must have been such a relief to finally be free of him and all of his ties.

As the house lay empty, I wondered about all of the events that led to him being taken away. I wondered what he'd done in his final moments for him to be taken out of the house in such a way. It's one of those things that most certainly can keep any of us awake at night, pondering *what if* and *what might be*, but there's no point really to do so, as the outcome will always be the same, always unanswered, and the story will always be unfinished.

One thing I do know is that he, most repulsively, will remain mad, ugly and evil in my opinion. I knew what he had done, in terms of the destruction he'd perpetrated on innocent lives, to his own family members, no less.

Wherever he is, whatever he may be, I truly hope he can never harm anyone again!

CHAPTER FOURTEEN

Stranger to Me

*Closure - like time suspended, a wound unmended, you and I.
We had no ending, no said goodbye.
For all my life, I'll wonder why.'*

Unknown

Diane

My father? My dad, Gene? Where should I begin?

A kind man, sometimes vocally loud, he could tell stories of the past for years. I appreciated his presence around the house, it was needed most times with my mother always being so fraught and ready to snap at any given time; she was the dud candy in the shop that hadn't quite developed in the way the candymaker had hoped.

Of course, what was left of the sweet was a pernicious, weakened little amount of broken candy, that any little touch or presence would cause to break, just cause it to go.

That, right there, was how I would explain my mother in a nutshell; my father tried his hardest to contend with her.

Yes, he had his own problematic ways, but it didn't help that his wife needed a constant eye kept on her for outbursts and outlandish behaviour.

He kept his patience as best he could, however, he also had a hidden temper.

I suppose my parents were the type of couple that hid things behind closed doors and sheltered everything from the eyes and ears of others. They liked to see themselves as middle to upper class and produced that life and existence.

Church on Sundays was a big part of this pretence and trying to sustain anything in life usually fails if it's not something you were intended to do as it never comes naturally or easily.

Easy definitely did not find my parents.

Along with their difficult times and troubles came my equally difficult upbringing.

What I learnt from my father though was what I thought all men to be and what I assumed them to all be. Self-delusion told me that they were all kind and gentle, quietly spoken, and treated you well. What I learned from my mother was not to be difficult in a marriage and not to be fussy in a relationship, just try to please, try to do your best to make your man happy and to love you, because I could never understand what my father had found or seen within my mother.

Why did he love someone so wrathful?

Why put up with a difficult life such as his?

I never fully understood the extent of the issues she had, rather that I had to put up and shut up, just like my father.

Gene would sit comfortably and quietly from time to time and my mother Elizabeth would burst into the room like a bat out of the sky, as if the night turned to day in a flash, squealing and trailing drama, just train tracked at her back, right into where Gene was sitting peacefully. Within seconds a big uproar of a dispute would unfold between the two of them.

He gave as good as he got but from what I witnessed, Elizabeth usually had the upper hand and held control of the situation.

After witnessing many of these moments, I lost total respect for both of them, though mainly for my father as I could never understand how he could take that abuse from her and how he never sorted it out and stopped her from being this way.

I'd had enough and I would get away from time to time and go to a nearby friend's house. I was enthused about watching their parents, and how they conducted themselves around my friends and me. Fortunately, there were never any disputes or fallouts, not when I was around, though who knows what might be happening behind closed doors. I just felt completely at ease in their company and enjoyed my surroundings. The atmosphere was relaxed and joyful, happy, with a sense of fun in the air.

My friends' parents seemed easygoing most of the time, it was nice to see and I felt happy around them all. Sadly, I would wish it was me in that situation; I wanted that to be my family and what I had grown up with.

I wanted only to see the good and never any bad, however, in my life, I always experienced more of the bad than the good.

On regular occasions I would go to my happy place within, imagining what it would've been like to have had nice normal parents and a hopeful upbringing. I'd sit, looking around the four walls of my room, allowing my eyes to slowly drift upwards to the ceiling.

I'd go into another place, another time, where I'd sit, imagining I could hear my mother laughing or singing in the kitchen while she cooked.

My father would enter and whisk her around in a gentle dance, they'd both laugh as they gazed lovingly into each other's eyes; happy, contented and, most importantly, in love.

Full of adoration they would turn as one, still bound tight in their strengthened pose, as they looked towards my brother and me, sending sweet words our way. We would all giggle and form a family group hug, the sort of hug that says, *'Everything will be okay, we are all okay and that's all that matters, nothing else, in this entire world.'*

My imagination would run away with me during these moments, as my thoughts were insatiably out of my control, I just so wanted my life to be like that. I needed that kind of happiness, all of that sweet kind love to envelop my being and hold, support and reassure me that it would all be okay.

Sanity is a rather important part of being a human being and I should have had the sanity of a child, not of an adult, not of a worrier and not of a young mum.

I just needed to be me, a child, free, growing up in a fun, quiet world where life was joy, trees were green, skies were blue, and sometimes silence was golden when I needed it. I needed my childhood and my teenage years to be like this dream from my imaginings - before it was all over.

My brother was an interesting young man. He was born five years after me. I think my mother had such a time of it with me, she didn't feel it necessary to have another child so soon after. My birth had been pretty hard going, it most likely destroyed the joy of bringing a baby into the world for my mother. I'd say she did suffer from some form of post-traumatic stress disorder, coupled with post-natal depression. Living through that, she must have thought it safer to put off any more pregnancies for as long as it would take. However, the joy of being a mother must have gotten the better of her, as she opted to go through it all again to bring my brother Steven into this world. He was a joy indeed and his birth was ever so effortless and uncomplicated; a complete turnaround from mine. It made being pregnant and giving birth a little smoother for Elizabeth, though she still suffered post-natal issues and never fully grappled with being one of those perfect 'to-do' mums, seen casually strolling along out in the open day, moving at a decent pace with the intention of having somewhere to go.

Most days my mother would be in a sweat-induced type of hurry, always rushing, pacing around full of stress and anxiety, fuelled with the worry of either being late or trying to be on time for anything.

The 'to do' mothers would prefer smart but casual dress; tidy and clean. Their children were perfectly asleep as if drugged, while they enjoyed walking and having time for themselves, some headspace. I don't feel that Carol ever had this. Oh God, she wanted it, even prayed for it. However, it was not her, it wasn't in her blood or her genes, she was a frantic and erratic swan paddling on the surface while paddling even faster and uncontrolled below.

Steven was a good baby; he was not too much trouble, plus he had the goodness of having me to play with and equally bring him as I helped out with motherly duties. My father was just quiet and still, as ever, he did not participate much in the upbringing of Steven, or mine for that matter.

He thought it was a woman's work, meaning my mother Carol

was left to perform the majority of the 'duties', or as she called it, the 'work'.

She was not just a mother simply caring for her two babies.

Morning times started off all right most days, however, there would be the odd one when Carol would be in the foulest of moods. I could spot the tension integrating throughout her muscles as her shoulders rounded and her upper torso stiffened. The seconds would tick by as the temperature of Carol's blood rose higher, the colour in her cheeks becoming redder with every pant and sigh of her breath.

A constant car crash would make me and Steven nervous and afflictive.

Once dressed and finally ready, after all, the 'carry on' as it was called, I would then be ushered through and out of the front door, ready to walk up the front path and head off to school. Forever dreading that walk, I'd be drowning in the feeling after what had previously and prior to my morning school walk occurred in my home - carnage and stress.

At 6 years of age, I experienced that tension and worry, and it was more than likely that I had the blood pressure of an 80-year-old.

Steven was in his pram, cuddled up with a soft blue blanket, crying loudly as he would still be tired and not ready after the morning had started loudly and abruptly. Yet the three of us were finally on our way to my school.

When we at last arrived, there was a sense of relief and completion.

I was also aware that I was about to be flung into another disaster zone, this time full of academics, that I simply did not enjoy at all, but who was I to judge? My father worked extremely hard to have me educated, attending a private all-girl school; I was to just get on with it and feel lucky that I wasn't being sent to a boarding school instead, as that would be my only other option if I kept up my moaning.

I hated all of it passionately, yet I did my best to remain quiet and get along with my co-students.

When Steven became of school age, my parents decided to send him to a boarding school. I could neither understand nor believe why they had arrived at that decision, although I secretly had an inner sense of delight at what I heard.

I'd always known that Steven was their favourite child.

Assuming that my mother and father had both had parents themselves, I thought that perhaps this decision came about as they had realised it was not correct to favour one child over another, and Steven was clearly no longer the favourite child.

Not that I was to be instead, I never was the favoured one. No, but I did feel optimistic that my relationship with my mother may now improve. Maybe this was to be the stepping stone we needed to rebuild it and our family, as a whole, would get better as well.

It did not.

As the years went by, my father got lazier and more useless; an accident at work saw him lose many of his skills. He had to make the hard decision as to what parts of the job he wished to resign from; essentially, he had to accept a pay cut. With this came the unforeseen money loss that my parents probably never imagined. They'd both been born into wealthy families and had always been secure in their personal accounts. Funds had never been an issue for them. Now, all of sudden, they had to watch their money and put aside bill payments. This created a senseless style as they rejigged all the things that they had never even had to think about in the past.

All the money just started to disappear, leaking out of the home - faster than water gushing down a drain after the plug gets pulled from an overflowing bath.

The household vibe and atmosphere became increasingly raw and delicate. My mother's already fragile state of mind and health worsened, as the financial situation brought in bigger blows and more damage.

Then, came the calm after the storm...

Luckily, my paternal grandparents came to our rescue and provided our family with the ever-so-needed funds to free us of our debts and to aid us in moving on to better, more hopeful, things.

Steven's boarding school was cut short and he was reinstated to a basic public school. It was difficult for him to move from a posh lifestyle to a normal mundane ruling of life with normal schoolmates and co-students. His childhood and, subsequently, his teenage life, suffered terribly due to all this.

In all of our mistakes in life, it is at the hands of ourselves that others will suffer; something that we forever repent in our dreadful moments of life.

My father blamed himself for all of the problematic and unescapable events. He had self-destructed with alcohol and other self-debilitating ideas, as he tried to find some resolution to how his emotions were frantically playing out in relation to all that had happened in our family life. However, what he did not realise was that absolutely none of this was his fault, nor was he to blame for anything, he had only ever done his best and what was right at the time for the family. I strongly feel that with his injury and loss of work, along with my mother's ever-failing and deteriorating health and state of madness, he found it all a tad too much.

I did not see him as the type to take matters of life and death into his own hands, granting he was clinically depressed.

Elizabeth never gave up the fight with her unstable and regrettable actions; she never let go of her hold upon her husband and the sum of what she concluded he was responsible for, which made for a very unhealthy recipe of ill failings and critical disputes.

I and Steven only wanted our parents to sort it out and repair all the damage that had been done. We wanted for time to heal itself and for the clocks to turn back and we wished that possible on so many occasions that we sat with our hands covering the lower part of our faces, holding in our involuntary reactions at what our parents vocalised to one another.

My dad became a stranger to me.

He was a stranger who was living in my house, a weird and quiet, yet still volatile man.

I no longer recognised him and what eluded this further from my notice was that my mother voiced several times that men all turn out to be like their fathers. If you want to know what a man would be like in the future, look at his father, that would tell you everything. If a man's father was a drinker, his son would turn out to be a drinker. If a man's father was a beater of his wife, his son would go on to beat his wife. If a man's father was an emotional abuser, his son would go on to emotionally abuse and so on.

Mother concluded, saying to me, "So, Diane, there you go, that's what a man does become, he becomes his father, and I can already see the signs of it within your brother."

The more she pinpointed these traits and faults, the more I internally stipulated what she could see and that I needed to see it for myself.

That was where it all began.

Steven started to embroil our mother into arguments, either with a backlash or words, and these rows stemmed from quarrels between our parents. Steven thought it was the right thing to do, to have his father's back, and to try to control the situation by putting our mother in her place - back in her box. Quietly but surely they tried to do just that and my mother's expression said it all. What she could see happening was not what she wanted for her only son. However, he was unrelenting in his ways and it seemed that, like Gene, like Elizabeth, like anyone in life, Steven had this behaviour pattern built-in and engraved into his genes and moulded into his blood.

It was already there from the day he was born, though what I had not understood at that time was that, yes, sometimes it is in your genes, in your soul, yet the people in your life, and especially the ones closest to you, can have such a great impact on your emotions and your essence, your eternal life.

You have to be careful what you let in and you have to stay controlled.

My mother never could do that and to this day my parents are still together, still muttering away with hurtful uses for each other. However, that is them, it's their marriage, and how they choose to behave.

As far as I am concerned, the family I was given and brought up with are all strangers to me and shall remain so.

CHAPTER FIFTEEN

Wonders and Wariness

To feel safe around someone's energy is a different kind of intimacy.

Unknown

Emily

I've never ever felt safe around men.

It's never mattered or concerned me what a man's age might be or what his personality might be like.

All I've known and ever felt was the non-safety aspect of their presence around me.

It just felt not right for me, in any sense or form, to be around them.

I wanted to be loved, I wanted to be happy and secure too. I wanted to be wanted and needed. I wanted to be content and at peace with a man, the man of my dreams; yet I could not and cannot seem to find that peace or that form of yearning in my own soul.

I have always felt lost and desolate, incomplete and useless, without a man by my side.

Often I've wondered, frustrated in my thoughts, on why my mind contemplated this matter, but still no answer or conclusion has arrived as to what exactly was the reason.

Perhaps I needed a psychologist? I tormented my head with these thoughts, useless and wasteful thoughts, but were they though? Perhaps it was exactly what I needed, someone to talk it all through with and come to terms with the fact that I've got problems. I wanted to cry, just to let it all out. My heart, my soul, the very essence of my soul was breaking, crying out for nurture and heartfelt companionship.

What if I never felt love or even companionship again?

What if I never had a connection again?

What if... what if... what if?

My very wise sister once told me about the '*what if*' monster and how if you delved into it, and thrived towards it, eventually it would get you when least expected and it will not be pretty. The '*what if*' monster sounded so stupid and so silly, however, it was very much true and I needed to stop - stop in my tracks.

I have to prevent myself from thinking about or conveying this matter any further. Stop the worry. I really wish I could. Instead, I veer into covering my eyes as well as half of my head with both hands, clammy from the situation that has arisen, or one that I had most surely caused. I would count to five or ten without any difference, no turnaround result, and no new option or answer. I would continue the repeated process of covering my eyes and head as if in a way to protect them both from the permeating trauma, the exposure of upset and demassification.

Would this precise useless moment ever end?

Yet at the same time something in my head spells, Is this *good? This is good, is it?*

I doubted that I was wholly in disagreement. Perhaps it was my head's way of telling me this was the breakthrough, this was the moment in which I would take back control and discover myself, discover truly what I was hiding from.

This was the moment I say, 'Enough is enough!'

Standing up, I'd remove the tight covering hands from my head and eyes, and say: '*I can do this, I am ready to uncover where I need to be and where I need to go next - what road or avenue. I am now ready to roll down into what's next.*'

'What is for you does not go by you,' that's always true, for the bad as well as the good, something most people don't realise in this life, this world. People don't realise those bad things are supposed to happen to good people for a reason, too. The reason I haven't yet been told or even decided what it could be, however, I just know that one day, far in the distance, I will definitely find out.

I used to use guys as much as I could for my own benefit and self-satisfaction. Not in a sexual way, in a type of redeemable way. I would use them at my beck and call when I very much needed them. For instance, nights out with the girls from university. Keeping in touch with particular individuals served well and endured fit for the purpose of carting me to and from wherever I needed to get to, usually from my home to Glasgow, then from Glasgow back home later.

Some people would indeed call this type of lifestyle unsafe and unruly, though I simply saw it as normal behaviour for a typical, cheap night out. It was just what I needed to get me up the road safely.

'Safely' - that must be the epitome of a joke.

There was absolutely nothing such as 'prime safety' in getting a lift home with a stranger.

Like, just what the absolute hell was wrong with me, thinking that I could get away with doing such things?

I was astonished and shocked myself by what I was possibly getting into, not only by myself but with some of my unwary friends too.

On one occasion, and I genuinely believed this wasn't my fault though I shouldn't have tried or concorded to entice a young man to do what I'd asked of him necessarily, however, it was his duty to provide me with care and a gentle approach and to get me home safely, as I had assured myself. It was one darkened summer's evening, when I was forlorn enough to ask this young man, albeit older than me at the time, to drive me home from a night out with friends in the city of Glasgow. He assured me that he would and could get me home, convincing me that it would be the right thing to do and the only option to take. Being a student on a lower set income, any opportunity that arose to save money appeared interestingly fruitful to my needs and I jumped upon it with every enthusiastic approach and intensity I should never have had. I met him through a friend of mine and I believed and secured him within the echoes of my mind to be reliable and trustworthy.

Having spoken to Andy multiple times via telephone contact and the occasional text message I had got to know him and I felt I understood him and his hardened personality. I wanted to be the one to tame him, reel him in toward the stability of my being. I wanted to bring him into my reality and place him in a concrete zone, with me by his side. However, my gut played a significantly different part in the story, as it told me all the answers I needed to know. My gut instinct was my only true friend and it was indeed the only thing I could trust. My gut told me 'No'. Plain and simple, it was to be a 'No'. Andy was a 'No'. Yet, did I listen? No.

I didn't accept what I felt as real. It was, to put it absolutely frankly, sheer and utter desperation for love and desire. If that meant it would be coming from just about anyone or would come from particularly anyone, then, unfortunately, despairingly and dangerously, that would be enough for me.

I had no thought process of it nor any sensible consideration of what exactly I was near about to get myself into.

As a young teen, I had no fear, most likely one of the only times in my life when I was both carefree and weightless.

Where I was unknown and unidentified. Real, but nothing and no one in this young subtle quiet life. Not one clue did I have as to the daring discoveries I was still to find and pull myself from and out of, saving myself and beginning a brand new chapter of life, setting out new boundaries within myself, where my life would change and adapt to new levels that I had never known existed.

I wish this was not the way or the end, however, I do mainly blame myself for the main diploidy in my life and I take responsibility for my stupidity, however, I do not take responsibility or ownership for what happened to me, or what I had to go through. I do not own what I had, which was the unfortunate ability to realise just what adolescence can reveal and introduce.

I was only 17 years of age at the time, old enough to know right from wrong though young enough not to understand that I shouldn't be going into the big bad dark world of nights out, drinking, partying and certainly not travelling home at all hours alone.

Going into Glasgow with friends for a night out was the complete norm for me and we had been doing so at every opportunity that arose. I found myself lucky that I must have looked old enough back then to have the fortuity to be allowed to enter over 18 establishments without the use of id to hand. I was never regularly asked for it, I'd say perhaps on two or three occasions but no more. I thought at the time that this was the best thing that life had to offer me to get in and out of pubs and clubs when I should have been at home safe and sound, head buried in study and essays that were due in class the following week.

A new dress picked out by hand from a regular shop I liked to use, along with new high-heeled shoes, a bag and a coat, all for the up and coming named night out. Preparation was key and I was always prepared. Fake tan, hair, makeup - it literally could take days in advance to get organised. I loved it, I lived and breathed for it, the whole escapade excited my bones and gave me cause for joy in my life.

Before I could truly get further excited and in the mood, I had my Saturday job in an exhibition centre where main photographers and artists would showcase their work. The Gallery of Modern Art was built over four floors, it housed a café and shop too and it was my ideal place to work as I truly enjoyed it on the inside. Sadly, I had a lack of confidence on the outside and struggled to interact, and attend to the customers who attended. My job role involved helping with the set-up for upcoming exhibitions, working alongside clients showcasing their work and liaising with customers. A lot of which I found rather difficult and mentally strenuous work due to my inability to talk to just about anyone.

Walking around shyly and with my head down during most of the day did not help me in any avenue of the job and I felt the presence and peering eyes of my employer heavily watching down on me, observing the difficulties I faced.

My day began at 9 am and came to an end at 4 pm, when I conduced a rather happy dance in my head to the tune of *'You can go now'*. I thought great I can leave now to grab my stuff and head towards the bus station, hop on a bus back home, before then returning to the city for my closely nearing night out. Most embarrassingly each Saturday around the same time, I had to run from my place of work all the way up Buchannan Street to the bus station in the hope I that had not missed my bus. There was a sense of relief when I entered the station to see my bus ready and waiting at its dedicated stop. Unfortunately, I had no choice, having to return back to my old life of getting buses. All of the nights out were causing my financials to take a deep decline. After all the bus was miles cheaper than the beloved trains.

The bus would take around 25 minutes to get me back home and from there I had a window of around two hours to get ready and head back out for the same bus to take me back into town where I would catch up with my friends, all of us ready for our big night out.

Our nights out were fantastic and utterly enjoyable, and I was fairly sensible with alcohol as I could be unlike some of my fellow companions. However, this one particular night was to hit me stealthily and shock me to the core with the unfortunate realisation that you cannot trust anyone, even the people you believe you can.

Andy, as mentioned before, was a guy I had spoken to for a while now and met briefly once. It should have been known to me what kind of person he was by the way he spoke and conducted himself, but I found myself in a rather lonely place, as of recent weeks I had not found romance or a partnership when I had been going out. I took to him and thought maybe if I gave him a chance, he may possibly be the man for me.

How wrong I was.

Andy was jumpy in body and nature; his tone of voice was gritty and he used slang. At times he would put me down, then laugh it off, calling me sensitive and saying I had no sense of humour. Sadly, he duped me into accepting his distinct and off-putting ways. I think deep down at the back of my youthful and naïve mind, I knew he wasn't right; he certainly wasn't right for me.

I would even go to the extent of saying that I didn't believe he was or ever would be right for any woman.

After my night out ended, it was around 1.30 am and I found myself at a loss to secure a local taxi to take me back home. Times became desperate and instead of continuing to wait outside in the cold like everyone else, I took it upon myself to phone a couple of different guys I was in talks with at the time, in the hope that one of them could rescue a damsel in distress and take me home safe and sound. It was of course Andy who took my call eventually after a lot of tussles and he offered to pick me up from town and give me a lift home.

When he arrived to collect me, I was so relieved to get off the cold street and into the warmth of his car that I felt an instant circle of security all around me and thought I'd done the right thing.

Wrong! How very wrong I was.

We chatted for a while as he drove slowly and carefully along the roads back home. I was surprised he hadn't been out or drinking as it was a Saturday night and he was only slightly older than me at the time. He was a carer for the elderly and when people have that line of career you always assume they are good people and they do the right thing by others. He was off duty that weekend and he had decided to stay at home which in one way was great as I had a lift to hand. In another way, I wondered why he didn't just go out like the rest of us.

Halfway through the journey, his nature changed slightly and his behaviour was off. He became somewhat despondent and, on a few occasions, completely ignored anything I put forward to ask him.

I found this a bit strange and at times hazardous, as I was alone in a car next to him, with him having all of the control in the driver's seat.

Eventually, we got closer to my house and I relaxed. I felt glad that we were approaching a place of normality and safety. We waited at some traffic lights which seemed to take forever to change when he asked me what I liked about him. It took me a fair few seconds to come up with an answer as by this point I felt a little insecure sitting next to him and had previously decided back at an earlier set of lights that he was not the guy for me after all. So I had to come up with a little white lie and said something along the lines of, 'Oh you are a little funny, I suppose.' Then I felt this feeling crawl all along the right-hand side of my body, this vibe that oozed from him over to me that he was not at all enthused by this remark, that this was not something that had given him cause for utmost relief. Instead, I think it angered him, perhaps he had heard it all before from another young girl he had lured towards him.

After a second or two of silence where he was dissolving and fragmenting the pieces of my words in his own unique frame of mind, he sat back in his seat, with a slight giggle and hum.

We drove through the lights as they had finally turned to green and he moved forward in first gear and crawled along the road another hundred yards, then he violently turned right without warning me or anyone else on the road - not that there was anyone - but that is beside the point.

We were now driving down a darkened road; in fact, it was completely pitch black.

I knew exactly where we were, however, at night it was so dark and isolated I found this an odd place for him to be taking me. During the day this place was an old industrial site, used by multiple car garages. It has the longest and darkest lane through it, starting at the main road and merging with a quieter road at the other end.

In the night hours, there wasn't a soul around and the darkness engulfs all of the buildings with complete isolation and emptiness.

Andy stopped the car and pressed the central locking system. He was the only one who could access it.

I hesitatingly asked him, "Why have you stopped here and what are you doing?"

To which he replied, "You know why…"

Well I certainly did not know why, though by this point I had a good enough idea as to the reason. He leaned over and approached me with the intention to kiss me.

I pushed him back and said, "No. I just want to get home. Please can you take me home?"

He rejected my requests and began heavily to protest, as he moved towards me for a reciprocated kiss.

Darkness loomed from his eyes and his overall being, but that may have also been because it was so dark in general.

I continued to push him away, though he was in no way relenting from his intention. My heart left me at this very point and lots of different things began to run through my head as to what may unfold next. I remember his force of being and how heavy he was, the raspiness of his voice growing increasingly heavier and angrier. I then found myself in a complete state of panic where my head was in the worst place and thinking the worst. I felt that something nasty was about to happen. Suddenly, there was a buzzing sound ricocheting from my bag that was in the footwell of the passenger seat at my feet. I managed to suppress him away from me and he played ball, allowing me to check my phone. It was my friend from earlier checking if I was okay, she was extremely drunk and I could barely make out a word she was saying.

The adrenaline fight or flight mode kicked in and I thought of a plan of survival.

No, I didn't think that this guy who is sitting in the driver's seat next to me is going to kill me or anything, however, I did have a slightly worrying feeling that he might do something else, which could have had devastating and lasting effects on my being for the rest of my life.

I knew I had to get away.

I began telling my comatose friend exactly where I was and who I was with. I told her that I would be there soon and not to worry etc, just to wait for me. Many lines of lies just shimmied out of my mouth down to the phone, all the while I was trying to keep what my friend replied on the down low, as I had to make sure that Andy did not hear a word of it.

Once again, I uttered, "Wait for me, I will be back soon. Phone me back in a minute and I will let you know exactly where I am."

I hung up the phone and urgently told him he had to return me home immediately as there had been a crisis with my friend; she had fallen out with her boyfriend and had showed up at my home address and was now waiting inside for me to return.

Whether or not this had any impact on his malevolent mind, I don't know, but he did the right thing and agreed to get me back home to her. My plan was working.

Andy started up the car and drove out of the dark lane, back onto the open road that was full of lights and houses, and he got me home. Of course, my friend was nowhere to be seen, but I insisted to him she was in my house waiting and I ushered him to unlock the door so I could go to her. I was free, ready to leave and return home. When I turned the handle of my front door I turned back 180 degrees and gave a small unenthusiastic wave. I entered the safety of my home with a heavy pain in my heart and my gut from the mistake I had just made.

I called my friend back, at this point she'd probably passed out with excess alcohol as she did not take the call. I was so relieved, glad and thankful to her as she may just have saved my life or at least some part of it.

I lay in bed with all the thoughts of the night, replaying everything that had happened with Andy, over and over. My head also disturbingly played with what could have happened and made me feel sick to my stomach, it added a crippling fear to my distrust of men.

If he could be like this, so could many other men surely!

I called my other friend Michelle the following day. She had me connect with Andy through her current boyfriend. I told her what had happened and she shot me down saying I had overreacted and I was being '*para*' as she called it, which was shortened for *paranoid*; she still uses that term even today.

However, she couldn't bring herself to believe that Andy was capable of anything like what I experienced with him the night before and our friendship almost ended over the situation. I knew that something deep in my gut, call it gut instinct or whatever, was telling me that Andy had more sinister plans for me that night if my other friend hadn't called me when she did.

A few weeks passed and my friend Michelle phoned me for a chat. I accepted and we chatted, quickly into the conversation she divulged to me something I will never forget and something that still haunts me to this day.

She said to me, "You know Andy and what you told me about that night he picked you up?"

I responded, "Yes."

Michelle continued, "Well, Andy did the same to another girl and he raped her."

I went into silence, shock and horror.

Michelle panicked and asked, "Are you there, Emily?"

I said, "Yes, I'm just shocked - now do you believe me?"

She replied immediately, "Yes, I'm really sorry."

From the night when he picked me up to the night he supposedly raped another girl, he had battled and burdened me with a call upon a call to try and get some form of contact with me.

For my safety and sanity, I refused all calls and texts from him, eventually, I deleted his number and avoided him at all times and it was over.

Never again would I trust in the same way and I certainly was weary of ever hopping into a car with some guy I had not had much previous contact with.

I was lucky though, I believe that night it was not just luck that saved me, it was some higher form of energy, some level of the unknown that we do not believe in. Perhaps someone or something from another realm, knew I was in danger and did everything they could to protect me that awful night.

I will always be thankful for whatever or whomever it was.

CHAPTER SIXTEEN

What I Never Knew

Stars cannot shine without darkness.

Anonymous

Diane

Work was hard, I found each day to be increasingly difficult, tiring, and wearing. It felt as though my mood was growing worse, a monster inside my head.

As the darkness became darker, the world became smaller and less meaningful.

I wished and longed for happiness, peace and everlasting stability for myself. The sacred space inside my head needed to be free. I needed to find a way out, to be set loose beyond the monster's grasp, the box, the space it was trapped in.

Did I need some intervention or help?

Did I need to evaluate and assess myself?

After all, I was a doctor.

The question of my mental state was one I argued about daily and one I wanted all the answers to, however, they never arrived. I never got the peace that I yearned and craved for. It felt as if I was chasing after a bus that never stopped; it didn't even slow down just a little to allow me some time to catch up, to get my breath back, to gather myself together, to compose my stature and to relax. No, this bus just kept on going, accelerating even faster and further into the distance, where it eventually became impossible to catch up with, to ever stop it, to ever climb upon it.

That was me, that is me, that is my mind. Empty yet full, dark with little to no light, unearthed, unfree with nothing in front or ahead of me to grasp onto. The days, weeks and months that followed became much worse, heavier and somewhat darker; truly, it became a living nightmare to regain any sense of sanity back. Some days, I'd say around a small handful of times I could see the bus in the near distance, almost close enough to begin the rerun all over again of trying to catch up with it. I'd thought to myself, '*I can do this, this time I will succeed. I can run, fight and complete what I set out to do today,*' only to end up feeling dumbfounded, as I would be left in a state of incomplete, uncontrolled emotion where I'd lost to that bus once more.

I decided at that point that I wouldn't try to beat it anymore; I wouldn't fight it anymore.

I would just let that bus go and I'd hope that I'd never see it in my line of sight again.

It was gone and it was never coming back.

Five Years Earlier

The question of children was still very much a prevalent issue in the minds of the many people around us.

I wasn't sure if there was a specific reason that I felt the way I did, or if that was a reason in itself.

Why would I not want to jump at the chance to have a child with Daniel, my husband?

After all, he was such a good man. He showered me and caressed me with love, understanding, and reassurance whenever I needed it. I loved him for that and I understood him, as he understood me.

It was all I'd ever wanted; all I'd ever dreamed of.

His job was going well, we were at a very good point in our lives. I had the added luxury of the fact that Daniel's parents and the majority of his family lived a good two-hour drive away from us and, due to that, we rarely had to see or deal with them. I wasn't the best at putting on 'an act' for family and friends. I am who I am and it physically drained the very life from within my soul to behave falsely towards others. Daniel appeared happy and content within himself and he was the type that didn't need anyone.

He did, however, need me, or so I thought…

Daniel wanted us to have a perfect life, just me and him, and this long-sought-after baby. We had great times together he and I. We laughed, joked, and ran around silly, we were young at heart. We felt free when we were together, enjoying each other's company. He was my husband and I was his wife, and I wanted to make him happy, and then I did.

At the older age of 32 and my Daniel now being 37, it was in the year 1975 when we announced I was with child and our baby was on the way. I was pregnant with a son, which of course I did not know at the time, and what I also never knew was how wonderful that was going to be, although my eyes at that time were close enough not to let me see that or anything else.

I felt a little scared and apprehensive as to what the future had in store for me. I just wanted to cry in a corner of our home, to be invisible even. Ignorance was my idea of reality and I was keen to ignore what was yet to come. Daniel was ecstatic and overrun with happiness. He had always wanted a child before we met, and with me, for a long time. Finally, this was his life now - perfect in his eyes, secure and complete.

"Let's look to the future," he said.

We had everything we wanted or could possibly want. I believed him with all my heart and soul, and my deep love for him. I could not get my head around how lucky I was to have such a supportive lover on my side. He was all I needed and wanted to get me through the hard nights of nausea and pain.

Pregnancy for me was not a joyous occasion and I struggled, but Daniel was there, helping me through it.

My family were fairly understanding too and they helped where they could, although my father called it 'woman's work', as he'd keenly urge me to just get on with it.

Some days I never moved much from the bed and Daniel would just laugh, saying, "Not to worry."

However, I was struggling, I wanted this part to subside. Eventually, it did and in February 1976 our son, James was brought into the world, weighing a wonderful 9lbs. In those days that was rather plentiful in weight for a male baby. He was a joy, we both loved him with all our hearts. Not long after he was born, Daniel had to return to his job as an engineer and I was on my own to get on with it all. This part was harder than anything, though I could never get my good old father's comment about 'woman's work' out of my mind. Things became harder and I suffered from post-natal depression, something that neither Daniel nor my own family could understand.

How could I be depressed when I had such a wonderful baby? He ate, he slept, and he was of the purest form of joy; I should have been relishing in this wonderful gift.

Sleepless nights and difficult days continued to brew the hate I had already broiled inside of me for Daniel, as I didn't think he could ever understand what I was going through. He tried, desperately he tried, in all of the possible ways he could to help, but miserably failed at every turn. He was merely useless and I just wished him gone some days, I wished he never return home. He always did and I would rest in relief and appreciation of having him home for some emotional support when there wasn't any at all on a physical level.

It was not a man's job to change, wash nappies, or feed and bathe the baby.

It was a woman's job.

My job as a doctor was a pressing matter away in the back of my mind, but slowly creeping outward into the front for attention. Due to the nature of my job and how much I was needed, I had to return when James was all but nine months old. My mother stepped into the scene, offering a helping hand to look after him to enable me to carry out my duties at the GP practice.

Every day became harder and harder as being away from

James was difficult, yet at the same time easy. Home life I found to be stressful and unorganised, yet it really should have been easier for me. When it came to going home, I would skip with joy to be returning there and the prospect of being able to unwind. However, any elation I felt was instantly shrouded by the realisation that being back in the marital abode with James and Daniel, and having to do all the work I was responsible for around the house.

Out of the ordinary mundane day to day life, Daniel began arriving home at a later time than his usual hour. As he began appearing later for dinner, at first, I didn't even notice as I was consumed with being extremely busy and fulfilling my usual duties.

Days, weeks and months passed vehemently and unsoundly by.

I would stand day and night looking out of my kitchen window at the lush forest with its green, dew filled grass, that lay still and silent in the back garden. The sun would be shining down onto specific areas of the garden, highlighting patches of the grass and lightening its colour to a golf course green. These sunny patches looked inviting and I often envisioned myself crawling onto them, stretching out on my back to gaze up at the sky. Something I used to do in my bedroom as a teenager when I lived with my parents.

The difference between the two periods of my life was that living at my parents' house I had been miserable, despite having a life, a home - even a bed.

In my married life, I had the grass, the garden and the sun, in the smaller quantities that were provided to me, yet I truly felt that my marital home was not my own. I felt as if I did not belong and that I could not escape this mundane life I was living.

I looked up at the orange, blinding sun, wondering in my own little head and the unenthused world, what it might be like to visit the sun, to actually go up there. Of course, it would burn severely, the heat and the burns would scold so bad, more than likely before I could even get close up to that much-needed worldly planet.

I wanted to be up there beside it, I wanted to feel the heat and the pain as it consumed my very being.

I wanted to do something no one else had ever done. I felt a connection to the sun, I wanted to be up there looking down, as opposed to what I was doing at that moment. I could no longer look at the sun, unless I wanted to permanently damage my eyes. I might never see them again - my child, my husband - or anyone else for that matter. The pain would be too much, the thought of never seeing what I needed to see again, well, that would be life-ending. I may be able to smell, taste and to hear better, but nothing could honestly compare to having plain sight.

I don't want to always see what's right in front of me because then there it is, the defined option of what I have to put up with, tend to, and deal with - sometimes that is just too much for me to cope with.

I continued to look out at the garden as I searched for hope to show me the way, for the sun to guide me entirely to the light that would fill me up, and for any answer to stay strong because right then I was not strong. I was weak, ever so weak, and tired, with a nine-month-old son, a job and a husband, all bearing down on me, it was just too much. Perhaps I needed a holiday, a nice warm family holiday. Maybe I should arrange something. My head inside was a constantly busy town full of people, rushing, bustling, organising and running around, it never gets a break.

Daniel arrived back home late yet again, his excuse being that work took longer than usual to depart from, but he is here now.

Yes, because that makes everything better and all okay, I thought.

I set aside my enraged emotions over his disappearing acts, trying to keep a small amount of positivity in my sights. I put across the idea of a holiday to him, to which he agreed to begin with and I felt relieved then. However, as quick as that relief and the excitement filled my body with energy, doubt and strain crept in slowly and fast too as if almost it was trying and slip in undetected.

I cottoned onto it straight away though, racking my brain for clues and answers as to why this was happening to me.

I realised that taking a young baby and a rather on-edge, workaholic husband away to another destination or country may turn out to be an exacting task, one that would require structure, dense organisation, and much energy, something in which I had been lacking for some time.

Why the need to actually go away when we have such beautiful surroundings here in sunny Dorset?

I pleaded my case with Daniel and we eventually turned away the idea of upping sticks and going on an informed holiday. This, of course, gave Daniel more stress to be added to his own soul and, as work grew, a bigger problem than ever.

The late-night arrivals started to get later and my workload grew faster.

Cooking, cleaning, organising, delegating, being a full-time mother, as well as a full-time general practitioner. I rarely saw or met up with any friends or family during this period of time, as I just managed to get through each day, increasingly with the hope that this delirious cycle would eventually come to an end. I hoped and prayed to anyone listening for time to proceed faster and for everything in my life to move beyond where it was then, allowing me to reach the next day without finishing the current or previous one.

I think that people who knew me could see that I was not coping very well; actually, it wasn't particularly easy to hide and my parents were quick to inform many around them of my difficulties, which made it all the more tiring to overcome what I was feeling. I knew deep inside that something was not quite right, though to actually pinpoint it, would be a whole other nightmare.

It was like trying to find water in the desert.

You search and search, going through every option and reason to find it, yet I still could not find that water - not even a single drop. Suddenly, out of nowhere, a river arrives, and then a sea, and violently at the end, a tsunami which ends all existence, stamping all over the very start of what you were trying to discover in the first place. My emotions and my moods were much like that scenario – exceedingly difficult to spot or understand, yet they were equally worried and unpredictable.

Who knew what could happen, or what I might do next?

Over the next year, small things with my husband crept in slowly but surely, and I found myself in an increasingly difficult circumstance with him as I wondered what was going on.

One day, I sat him down to go through things and I asked him how he was feeling. This is not something men would be willing to participate in back in the 70s, but I felt it appropriate and somewhat urgent and I had to get to the bottom of what was happening with him, what was going on with us.

As most husbands are inclined to do, Daniel shrugged things off, and threw me the 'work has been difficult' line, it was so busy and tiring, and he was trying his best.

I felt sad for my husband then, as I worried about what all this stress might be creating for him and what effects my behaviour and uncontrolled emotions were having on him, his health and, most importantly, his happiness.

I wanted him to be happy again like he used to be, he always had the most wonderful smile and I felt he needed to regain that smile and to have his joy returned.

Daniel and I used to have an amazing relationship before James was born.

I often concluded that it was something to do with the bringing of our son's little soul into this world that was somehow responsible for the destruction of our marriage.

We were soulmates Daniel and I, after all. We only had each other him and I, but now there were three of us and it was so damn hard, time-consuming and difficult. I tried my best to overcome my affective mood disorder, I was enthused to be happy, and sometimes I even lied although it was hard to deceive Daniel as he always knew when I did.

Even James picked up on some of the emotional content and his temperament changed with the course of it all. Daniel expressed to me just off the bat that he had been confiding in a work colleague about some of our struggles. I was instantly shocked, hurt, and I felt betrayed that he could do such a thing, divulging our secret business. Exploring his feelings and emotions with another woman.

This brought out jealousy and affected me quite strongly.

I closed down on him after that as I became increasingly concerned about what sort of nature his chats were with this colleague. I wanted to know exactly what they may be saying to one another, or how she was supporting his needs, wants, and how she was trying to refute his sadness. One day I discovered a little note from her in his lunch box.

She wrote, "You can do this, keep strong."

I was horrified and exceptionally angry, I was in complete despair.

How could he?

How could any man?

How dare he do this to me!

My anger soared through the room like a fireball simmering to the point of explosion, only escaping through open windows or cracks in the walls. I had hoped the neighbours had not heard of my dramatic, expressive outburst.

Please just will all this stop, can it all stop?

Is it too late to be fixed?

Once again I questioned Daniel and it felt like an interrogative interview for him, most likely, but it had to be done, things had to be said so they were said by me mainly. I had to know just exactly what he was up to, what kind of game he thought he was playing at. The hurt grew into a potent bitterness deep within that was harder than ever to control, or to even to slow it down.

When I looked at him I felt nothing but hatred.

My husband explained to me that he needed someone to talk to and surmise his feelings with, and his thoughts too, before they all boiled over into nothing because that's what he may feel towards me by the end of it all.

Nothing? Was that all I meant to him?

It hit me hard just exactly what I was doing to him and how much I needed to regain a grip on this life and take a reality check. Daniel and I knew we could simply no longer continue on in this way; I certainly could not. My behaviour was an outrage, it needed to be steadied on its path. Deep down I knew I could not contain it forever or stop it completely. It was if there was a little demon inside of me that needed to escape and come out, allowing everything to be real and to be what it needs to be. I could not keep up this pretence any longer.

We sat down together over dinner and put pen to paper in order to write out our plans for the future as to how we would overcome our current issues and further to resolve our problems, upsets, and never-ending disagreements.

Daniel just couldn't go on with me behaving as I was, for much longer; it had affected him too much. My husband needed me to get on with things, awaken myself, and live my life - all he wanted was for me to be happy.

We arrived at the decision that I would give up my beloved job as a GP and turn to the occupation that was homemaker/stay-at-home mum. I thought this was much of the only choice I had and it was the best one to make for now. There was always most certainly the option to go back to work when I was ready. For now, I was not ready for anything, life was controlling me and taking over my everyday living when I should have been in control of it, of myself. The more I thought about working, the harder my days became; for the moment I had to put the idea of work and all that comes along with it, out of my head, and focus on Daniel and James. They were all that mattered.

I would keep our family house organised, tidied, ready, and filled with love.

I managed this for a couple of months and over that short span of time I became lingeringly unwell with one ailment after another. So many viruses were going around and having a young child it was no wonder my health was at such an all-point low. My deteriorating health became a difficult issue in our marriage once more. Berating all that we were and degrading my sense of self-worth and independence.

Just when would all this end?

I could only ask the question because the answer was unknown but likely inevitable.

CHAPTER SEVENTEEN

All You Can Do is Try

We are all after something that makes the empty spaces in us make sense.

Faraway

Diane

As more time lapsed, the further dishevelled and tired I grew. I also grew incredibly impatient.

I could feel the fight inside me raging about like a wild animal in captivity.

There was no lease of life to get to and engage with, just constant disappointment and strain, brought on by my inability to get better and my lack of good health.

Why me? Why me?

I ask that question over and over, looking and listening for signs and whispers as to what the answer could be, what it may entail, and any such way I could define and understand just what the hell was going on.

Oh, I could scream, let the wailing out from every crevice of my body to expel the pain and torment.

Screaming, releasing all into the open air and the free and wondersome life that surrounded me. Or, as some people suggested to me, the wonder of some free life that I might choose to believe was there.

Me, myself and I would simply sit there together in self-pity at that very day-defying thought.

I don't want to grow any older in this way, I cannot reach my baby, I cannot reach my husband, physically yes, that is also an issue, but metaphorically they, Daniel and James, they are just unfortunately distant within my capture.

I needed to capture them so I could have them with me forever and at all times, *Please remain by my side Daniel and never ever leave me.*

Daniel portrayed that he was great and all that I needed, yet it was all a cover-up; instead work and his little freedom were what got him through his compelling days. The days with me spent worrying about me, just how much more could he take on board or handle?

I often tortured myself with continuous inner questioning.

Do I think he may decide to leave me? Leave us, James and I, all alone and, if so, how would I cope? How could I do it on my own? No job now, no money, no freedom. No help around the house; no one to be there just for comfort.

I destroyed myself with these thoughts, painting myself with the belief that they could actually become a reality.

What if they did, what if, what if.

Just stop, that could never happen, surely never. I couldn't bear to be alone; I had felt alone my whole existence before my marriage and I wouldn't cope well with being alone or living without Daniel. I needed to get better for him and our son, I just had to try. Trying appeared to be the likely choice, however, it was frustratingly difficult as each time I tried, each time I tried so damn hard, I'd been knocked back again with hardship and worrisome failure.

This failure had an extremely detrimental effect on my state of health, Daniel could see I was worsening. He became difficult toward me, strange and somewhat just off. A hard thing to imagine and, even more so, to explain. I wanted the warmth of his love desperately, I needed nothing more in this life than to have him hold me tight and never let go.

I missed him even though he was right there, though I know he won't be for much longer.

I could tell he was leaving me, he had already left in his mind, he was going, further and further away from me, from us. The crying sound from little James' mouth was piercing and sharp, it affected each pore of my body. I wished it would stop, if only Daniel was here to help to get me through this. I needed him so much.

How had I become this way?

Once I'd been strong, contained and intelligent individual, yet now I was a shrivelling, sad wreck, alone, struggling, all in my decaying mind.

Where had my independence gone? How could I get it back?

I made the decision in my head that it was over, it was not coming back - my strength, my energy, my life. It was completely over. I couldn't see a way out of all this. And then possibly the worst thing that could have happened, happened.

Daniel left me.

He actually left me and of course James. How could he? How could he do this to me? He evidently had suffered the predicament for as long as he could; enough was certainly enough for him. How dare he though? Since when did he become so selfish and inherently distant, so embroiled in self-contained emotion? At the very time when I had needed him the most in our life together, he had left me. This, in turn, massively affected my state once again and lessened my ability to cope.

His leaving left me deranged, worried and manically depressed.

I needed him to return. James was now insanely out of control and I was unable to give him the stability and love that our son needed and deserved. Wishing endlessly that Daniel would come back to me, I found myself completely cocooned in a world that was quiet, still and empty. It was bitterly cold and I doubted in my mind and soul that any warmth would appear once again. I could no longer try and I was belittled by so-called friends, family and colleagues about my deteriorating weight.

I could easily lose a stone in a week and it was all so noticeable in my overall body appearance. Each time I put any form of food into my mouth, my stomach would flip over so excessively that my palate would become parched and irreversibly dry. At this point, I could no longer eat.

This whole experience left me withering away to almost nothing.

I needed Daniel to come home now, to save me, before there was nothing left and I was gone. If he did not come back to me then I must go. Days whittled away and at last in came the long-awaited contact from my husband. No apology from him, he simply wanted to talk and there he was within a matter of time back again in our home. Back where he always sat and returned straight into his old ways and habits. It was as if he had never left. I couldn't believe it and thought that my eyes were deceiving me. However, it was real, here he was, back where I needed him.

The very next day he left again following his old routine. Completely back to normal, we were once more in our organised life. Yet I was alone. Stuck at home all day with a crying son and struggling to get around. I decided I had enough of being at home, I needed to get out of there. I dressed James and put him into his pram, all wrapped up, as there was a fair breeze in the morning air. I took him to Dorset cliffs way above sea level.

It was a special moment between us as it was very quiet and peaceful, the two joys I enjoy about life the most.

When it's too quiet I often struggle just as much as when life is chaotic, however, at that moment and time it was all worth it. James slept as I enjoyed the fresh air. I watched the world go by and the seagulls loomed around in the hope of receiving some starchy, filling foods. The sea rippled gently in and out with the current beneath and the wind in the air gave it a helping hand. Other mums pushed their little ones around in strollers as they also enjoyed the scenery. The sky was bright and blue, with small fluffy white clouds - just enough of them to decorate the sky with another colour other than the usual old and dull hues and tones. I felt ecstatic at that moment; there genuinely was nothing better and then it hit me again like a train coming from nowhere and battering into my frail and lithe frame. Instantly I was reminded that I must go back. Home, back to that house.
That house, where it had all begun, carried on and came to an end.

That house is what forever haunted my emotions, feelings and intonate actions. I dreaded the mere thought of returning there and as my anxieties grew, James' cries and wails became louder than the crashing waves below us. I had thoughts at that moment. That was probably when I was at my absolute loneliest. I looked beyond and saw many other families, their mothers happy and admiring, in sheer delight, their little ones.

I could not understand why I was lacking in these feelings.

Perhaps we had rushed it having a child, although I'd waited as long as I could until I was ready. Daniel had pushed me fairly into having James when I knew it was possibly something I never could have wanted.

God, I punished myself over and over, very rarely did I ever give myself a break from this mental torture that I continued to put myself through.

If I could've only stopped thinking, just for a second. *For one second could it all just stop*, was my inward plea. The thoughts pushed on, shoving through every electrical cell and nerve in my brain's activity and within the fibres of my body. My body twitched with the non-stop overthinking and never-ending analysis. I would've very much liked it to stop immediately. It could not.

I returned home and stopped in at some shops to pick up needed items from the grocers. The usual things are bread, milk, and dinner items. All the while James was crying for unspoilt attention and love, crying for a mother who could. Crying to be held and wanted. My selfishness prevented me, instead, I held onto the loaf of bread for comfort and looked deeply into the eyes of the lady behind the counter who was putting the shopping through the checkout. I looked at her as if asking for the help of some kind, compassion, even advice. There was nothing, instead, she peered back at me, her eyes piercing through mine. I could tell just exactly what she thought of me, what she had conjured up in her small mind about me and my mothering skills. More than likely opinionizing and coming to the conclusion that I must have post-natal depression. That's what it was.

Part of me wanted people, strangers to think this, as they might be able to understand then why I was unable to deal with my own child, that I couldn't go to James when he truly needed me, that bread was of more importance than my son's soft and gentle skin, the warmth of his tiny body, the sweet baby smell that just lingered on forever and you couldn't buy or replace that smell.

I loved my child, I genuinely did, I just did not know how to show it to him.

I needed someone to tell me, directing me, controlling me almost. Was I just a living robot in this life? Perhaps, with no processing system. Emotional yet emotionless, strong yet weak and in need of direction. I know who had the remote to me though. Daniel did, he knew just exactly what buttons to press, what parts of me were working and which ones no longer did. He knew how to work me completely and without him I was nothing, no one, and I did not have the first clue how to work myself, how to fully function or move forward. When I thought about that I realised just how sad it was - that I am nothing without this man.

How had I ever coped or lived before him?

And why was it now that I needed and relied on him for so much?

Question upon question, never-ending.

Is it because of James? I asked myself, *Perhaps James is holding me back from being who I want and need to be.*

Maybe without James, Daniel and I would have the life we'd always dreamed of, instead of the tears, pain and noise, night after night. No wonder my husband upped and walked out because at that moment that was exactly what I wanted to do.

I wanted to park up this pram, leave the stupid shopping, groceries, whatever, and just walk out, walk away completely, except with the difference that I did not want to return.

Gathering my things together, I started on the long walk back to the house. The wind seemed to groan and flow faster through the air than it had earlier and the sky turned from inviting blue hues to a darkened grey and white. It was as if the clouds had decided to collect together right above me, and James in particular, they just hovered there for as long as they could until they decided to allow all of the rainwater they were holding to just completely billow down on top of me. There was now a stealthy dark vibe within the atmosphere and I couldn't help but now blame myself for this change in the weather. All my moaning and crying, the depression, the negative thinking, had no doubt caused this; that saying was true, the one about you having a *big black cloud* above you. Well in my case I did have one indeed, except it was not happening on all levels, however, in the metaphorical sense, it was in my physical reality happening right then.

Please don't rain down on us, I muttered, while I desperately hurried along as fast as we were able to go.
All the while overthinking all I had to do when I returned. All the household chores, putting the shopping away, dealing with James. Dealing with James felt like a chore as it was

sadly something I never enjoyed. That must be the saddest comment you could make about your loving innocent child; however, if I were to be honest with myself, I'd never enjoyed it. I suppose I'd never enjoyed him. He looked up at me with the deepest yet unhappiest eyes that were just crying out for some love; instead, I looked back down at him as I passed on my anxieties and stress about having to look after him, my own son. I truly wondered at times just what was wrong with me and why I could not change the way I was. The more I thought about it the worse it seemed to get, so I would bury my head further into the sinking sand hole I'd created.

Suffocating myself with my doubts, thoughts and never-ending worry.

Finally, I arrived home with only a drizzle of rain on us both and I was surprised to find Daniel back home early from work. This was a surprise albeit a nice one, as he was usually the opposite and late most days. We hugged and embraced each other while I came at him verbally with a cannonball containing the breakdown of my day. Daniel instantly looked aghast and I knew he couldn't handle hearing much more, once again. He didn't want this; I think all he wanted was for me to be happy like I'd been in the beginning, for me to recover my confidence and to simply enjoy my life like I used to.

All I wanted was for my husband to hold me and tell me it would all be okay.

Tell me I was strong and I could do it. He would tell me some things I wanted to hear every now and then, however, he didn't give me much hope or encouragement, this would be particularly evident in the tone of his voice, which would be flat and dull, yet with just a hint of zest to give me a small slither of the positivity I craved.

Nothing was ever good enough for either of us.

I harassed and devastated my mind with dangerously harmful and worrisome thoughts, telling myself over and over that I was not good enough, and that I did not deserve a life or happiness of any kind. I served myself brutality, telling myself that I should not have a husband or a child, or even a home. Instead, I should go and rot in some hole some place, where I'd never be discovered or found to be habituating there.

On the way back that day, as usual, I'd been looking around at everyone else, observing then judging, and fostering wrong opinions about them all, that they were thinking things that weren't even true, or that were any part of normal life.

Walking along, I'd believed that strangers passing by and thinking: *'who is she', 'what is she', 'she's not right not normal', 'a mess, odd, strange'. 'Definitely needs help'.*

Yes, maybe I do, please help me where needed, I thought in answer to these make-believe questions. *But where is this help?* I asked myself and I believed truly there was none available to me. To be seen as needing help, in my experience, meant you were seen as weak, mentally not well, insane even, potentially needing some sort of involuntary assistance from a psychiatric team. It was downright impossible and refutable to even have such thoughts enter into one's mind and knowing, truly knowing there was nothing you could do to get some help or attention for the very way you felt, only made matters worse.

Weakness to them, to all of them, was seen as useless, unworthy and wasteful and I thought that even Daniel was in agreement.

I believed my husband felt the same as the other people did on this matter and that he couldn't understand for the life of himself, why I was so unable to get it together.

I could smell the dense, dull air, it made me feel sick. I felt even more alone. I wished that I could be truly happy, though I believed then that it would never happen. It wasn't that I didn't want to be happy, it felt like something that I wasn't allowed to have so far in my short life's existence - I mean, why would it be?

Everything in my life to that point had only brought me endless misery, heartache and sadness. There was nothing I could do that would improve the way I felt. Not even little James could return the smile back to my face.

As the smell in the air grew thicker and denser, I knew a storm was coming.

The next day I travelled to Lulworth Cove with James snug in his pushchair. You can always tell, near the sea, when things are about to take a turn, as the sea grows a little angrier and the sky caves in on itself. Everything happens in quick motion; the sky swirls around the fluffiness of the clouds drawn in jagged edges, the darkness swarms and the sea forcefully rushes in to cover the shore. Waves crash and lap up the side of the Dorset cliffs, onto Lulworth cove, onto the beach, where I'd first met him. Daniel.

I reminisced about what once was, how I had escaped the despair and run into the joy that was a life with him, a marriage with him. However, at that moment, I still suffered in silence, I was saddened and meticulously unsure as to what to do about it all. The thoughts, the past events, everything came fiercely into my mind on that beach as I watched the waves growing harsher. It seemed like a replica of my emotions, all in that moment.

Wondering how, why, when, and what if.

I loved him I really did, but this nagging doubt somewhere deep within my stomach, within my soul told me differently, told me that have I made a mistake.

I was not a stupid girl, so what had led me to do such a thing?

Love, lust, wonder and confusion.

At that point, James became extremely unsettled, between the unpredictable weather and myself, his mentally unwell mother, my son was surely sensing and absorbing all sorts of feelings within his little self. Upset, tired, and hungry, my son needed love and reassurance. Something within me felt that I needed to go back and try again with Daniel, just one more time, just one more day. One day at a time, as other people always said, I honestly hated that line - *take one day at a time, it makes it easier*. No, as a matter of fact, it does not; it makes it harder. Didn't everyone just want to skip and jump to the good part? I know I did and the fact I did meant there was hope, meant there was still the fight within me to carry on and to find that inner strength. Perhaps I could do this, after all.

Maybe I was the strong one, despite what Daniel might have thought or believed; despite what his work colleagues or friends wished to think of me as they filled my husband's imagination and his head with deceptive mind plays that had been set upon my character.

If I could just get through tonight, get home, get dinner organised and ready, keep little James happy and settled, and hold Daniel at bay, then I could get through that night, which would lead me to tomorrow. I could start again, see what's what in the morning, afternoon, and tomorrow, the night would be over.

My days consisted of this repeating over and over, as I ran on a continuous hamster wheel that spun slowly around, unenthused and uncharmed.

Same shit, different day.

Would it ever change, could it ever change?

I needed to know.

CHAPTER EIGHTEEN

Sunshine in the Morning

The pain of yesterday is the strength of today.

Paulo Coelho

Emily

I never thought it would happen to me, life.

Life's greatest achievements, its greatest accomplishments.

No, not for me, although somewhere deep inside, lingering and festering away, was this urge and fire within me to fight back and say, *No I can do it, I can actually in the whole matter of fact, achieve anything my heart desires.*

Sounds a bit cheesy and predictable, yet I genuinely knew from that point on that I must set out to find what would complete me. My first port of call, or accomplishment as I liked to call it, was to have a business, reach the top of my game, be the one in charge and the best in my field. Photography was my thing, my career game.

How would I succeed in making it to the top of my profession?

First of all, I jotted down some thoughts and ideas.

Point one: I could become a lecturer and give way more enthused opinions and passion than any of my previous teachers from the school of doom, the dreaded university. I could make it fun for my students, intriguing, and inspiring them with all the things I'd wanted in their place but had only managed to endure.

Point 2: I could try to climb to the top and become a top celebrity photographer or photo stylist. That would be fun, however, potentially it would be an impossible dream to manage or even come close to achieving.

Point 3: I could open, establish, and run my own empire. My very own business - all for me, my dream, my goals and my desires. This one was my choice; I took the leap of faith and made the grand decision to take the plunge into the world of business. I accepted right there and then that it would not be easy or something that I could sail through, however, I strangely knew all of the loopholes and guiding lights to get me through the first difficult stages.

My mum was very supportive of my chosen profession, although I'm sure if she had had her way, she would have hoped for me to go into the spiritual side of life, to make my way into that very different and exceptionally multi-layered universe.

Who knows, perhaps I would go back to that area at some stage, though not just yet, not right now. I wanted to get on my feet first.

Before I knew it, the business was fast on its feet and I had made great headway with all the things I needed to do at the beginning to get things going. I attended vastly helpful business start-up classes while enjoying and feeling at home during this new learning curve.

Before Christmas of 2012, I'd found the perfect little shop to begin my new adventure in. It was a bit of a hellhole I must admit, utterly filthy and most certainly not fit for purpose. However, I received much help and encouragement from my sister to get in and get on with it, make it new, clean and ready for the opening in the New Year. In the meantime, I kept my work on the side going as I had to keep the money rolling in. It meant I could be wholly comfortable when I checked the status of my bank balance.

The days and weeks passed by and things became harder as there was just a little more work than necessary that needed to be done in the shop. I felt as if I'd bitten off more than I could chew at that point. Doubts and worries crept into my mind and I began to wonder if I had done the right thing after all. I had to stay positive, there really was no going back as I had signed a rental contract with the landlord, I could not give up or walk away even if I would have liked to.

I'd say I am not a giver upper though I am lazy. I'd rarely be up for a challenge, especially the decorative type one. I'd prefer not to go down that route and I would rather sit back allowing other people to do the job for me.

Some days I felt like crying as the stress and tension overran my body and emotions. It liked to break me down or rather I liked to allow it to do that. Perhaps when I let it in that's when I felt I got the break or recuperation that I truly needed.

While the works were going on within the shop premises, public interest was building and gathering from outside. The shop was in an affluent little town called Milngavie, and let's just say the people there were a different kettle of fish altogether. Privileged and entitled, or at least they believed themselves to be for the majority of the time. A lot of attention came generally from the most entitled ones, I tended to find it was the women who had come from nothing and met a rich husband, those were the ones who would take over and become the boss of all. For sure, they were the ones with the worst attitude and temperament.

Unfortunately, you really had to beware of these types of customers.

As I was still rather young when I started my business, consequently, I found that people didn't take me seriously. This was an issue that I'd fought against for most of my life. I would constantly be left wondering if people would take me seriously in spite of my young age. I hoped they would not judge me due to my youthful looks and my naivety. I did find that I took many things to heart at the beginning and I let them affect me, instead of shrugging them off and aiming them back at the darn soul that sent it my way in the first place.

Eventually, I did begin to wonder if these types of people had such a perfect, entitled and wondrous life, and why they were so miserable and nasty to innocent bystanders.

Shocking and absurd to say the least, however, I was never the type who'd take things to heart until after the abuse had set in. I would find myself in the middle of many disputes and arguments with said people, and women in particular, that I tended to clash heads. These sorts of instances didn't do much for my confidence and self-esteem and after a while, my anxiety levels increased where they'd been mainly stable beforehand.

I had not had much trouble in the past with this emotion called anxiety.

It almost feels as if it should be named as a 'someone' or an individual, for it seems as if it is 'someone' who constantly attacks you mentally from all corners and at all costs.

I could not afford any more knocks. It obviously started off slowly and built up into complete combustion where its full effects impacted my very core within. I steadfastly tried hard to stop anxiety in its tracks in an effort to prevent it and get over it just as quickly as it had appeared in my life. However, nothing helped, I was unable to restore myself back to the stable, healthy and normal individual I once had been. Most definitely this saddened me to the extent that I found it difficult to be myself in new and strange situations.

Who was I now?

What, or just who, had I become?

'A no-one', or at least that was the degraded putting title I enjoyed placing upon myself. As if things weren't bad enough without me adding injury to insult to my very own self. Selfish, in denial, and lacking complete and total worth at this point, I relegated myself to a shadow that lurked around in the background. I needed a planned yet unplanned, and narrowly discovered escape, I just needed to escape.

I hounded myself over and over.

Honestly, I actually felt unreal in that world and society at the moment of time I was living in.

When I spoke to potential contacts and clients, the anxiety and desperation of wanting to be normal, successful, and accomplished would rush over my upper body like hot toxic lava pouring from its previously psychotic-infused, episodic, volcanic eruption.

God, it burned and ached, then burned some more, all while my décolletage and face developed an unconcealable, bright red rash, that screamed, shouted and aggressed 'anxiety attack' all over it!

Ugh, at this point, was there any point left?

Well, yes, I still had a business to run, I had a client to sell my products and my work to all, which was most important. I hoped and prayed that they would look past my faulty humane default to my reaction of being under severe duress. Nevertheless, I carried on with the best performance I could and remained at little, and at best, one per cent positive at this point, with utmost hesitance in my being. All I needed to cure this disposition was a break or a holiday, I told myself over and over. If I could just get away for a little while, I could return infused with prowess and a new sense of joy, strength, and a determination to reinvent myself for everyone around me.

I did enjoy a holiday not long after with a good friend of mine that had gotten me through many years in my life. While it was all doom and dark grey clouds back home in Scotland, on the holiday I was warmed up, brighter and even happier, with the sunshine that began in the morning and continued every day in wonderful Greece. A full week, was bliss, sheer bliss. Some days yet remained the same, with the thoughts of an uncertain future, the uncertain hopes and dreams, I would be constantly pondering about whether or not where I was in my life was what I really wanted.

Could I do things differently or change something?

What was I actually working towards or living for now?

As the thoughts spiralled, suddenly I realised I was immersed in huge doubt, and submerged in regret over my current life choices. I needed to take charge and do something about this, I needed to try to fix myself and turn things around. Easier said than done. However, somehow I managed it, and there I was back in charge of myself and my flailing life. I had it again, I got back control!

However, just when I thought I had a clear and working handle on things, the irreversible and unforeseeable happened.

The accident was a life-changing incident for me; one that I would never forget, mentally or physically. My shop, the workplace and the surroundings that were already failing me emotionally and mentally, causing all the stress and budding anxieties, delivered yet another knock to bring me back down to earth, literally.

I would never forget that day.

Stupidly and unconsciously I recalled climbing upon an unsteady work counter to fix something within the upper part of the shop. Looking back, I think someone took over my body and made what I'm about to say next occur. While up there I felt rather safe and secure and nothing should have exceeded that during that moment, however, while in complete contention I felt as if someone threw me off balance aggressively. With a sheer slither of evil, I was sent crashing down from the worktop I stood on to the floor beneath. I crashed onto the wooden flooring with some effect and an almighty bang. I must have blacked out as I don't remember much about it, other than coming to and experiencing the searing pain shoot through my limp body, in particular, I felt it in my back. From that very small moment with a big effect, it was when I knew something extremely serious was wrong, but I still had the denial aspect then which kept me slightly hopeful.

It was like walking through a tunnel guided by a light, only to find that the light was a bulb which was rather dim, in fact, about to expire; that was exactly what it felt like then and afterwards when I discovered truly what was the issue.

The revelation was that I had not suffered as badly as I'd first thought. However, a check-up with the doctor revealed that I had caused discs within my spine to slip, as they call it, or even more so, in medical terms – to bulge.

As far as I'm aware, fluid-filled discs sit between each vertebra within the spine, they help with movement and keep the spine moving freely.

My discs, particularly the ones at the bottom of my back, were aggravated with the impact of the fall, which caused them to bulge outwards severely, and to tap my sciatic nerve. This resulted in an immediate weakness within my back and spine, as well as the nerves that sprouted out from the upper body going right down to the lower body.

I could only describe the weeks and months that followed that fall, as sheer hell on earth.

I felt as if I would never progress through that horrific time, all the while trying to pick myself up with thoughts similar to *Well, there are people worse off than me. There are people who've had accidents that can no longer walk, or there are people with a terminal illness. I'm sure given half the chance they would give a limb to only be suffering the way I was after my life-altering accident.*

Despite thinking these things over and over and trying to heal my mind emotionally to detach from what had occurred, nothing could or would stop the pain I was feeling. Numerous trips to and from the local GP saw me on vigorous and manic medications that caused further trouble for myself in my own life and, more worryingly so, for others around me, loved ones and friends, who absolutely did not deserve the sheer aggression I caused them. Five months later and well into a drug that could only be described as 'a horror film', I was a changed person.

No longer was I the happy-go-lucky, slightly anxious, worker, I was now a complete breakdown of a mess; nothing and no one could sort me out.

I had to take ample time away from my work and I hoped that my business could scrape by on its own without me to steer it, it was like sending a ship to sea without its captain. Without complete stupidity, and possessing some sensibility, I realised that it was necessary to hire a younger photo graphist now. Someone not long out of university barely graduated, would be perfect. I did not want to see my business suffer due to my long absence.

Although my new employee had little experience, I allowed her to come up with the goods all on her own. Meanwhile, I sat back from the helm, at home, wallowing in self-pity and hitting the self-destruct button as I tried to figure out and recollect why this had happened to me.

I do remember that in all of the blurred vision and hope that I suffered with back then, someone made a comment to me and it has always resonated with me as it made complete sense.

On hearing and learning of my hurt, pain and suffering - because boy oh boy, was I suffering in that moment - that lovely human being told me the following:

'Never ever feel bad or guilty that you are crying over your pain because there are others worse off than you. Everyone's own suffering is unique and just as painful to the sufferer. So cry those tears, feel that pain and, yes, feel a little sorry for yourself to a certain extent, because without doing all of that, and without feeling and living through the negative emotive state, you will supress yourself, and that can cause more trouble in the years down the road. Let it all out and then regroup your emotions, your being and your soul, then live again to see another day and you will be free of it all.'

I kept in touch with my business and with my young inexperienced employee, who turned out to be rather more experienced than I had first thought. She was doing incredibly well and the work and sales were vastly coming through, to my pleasure. When I think back, strange and unlikely things were happening within that small shop that I was renting for my business and they only got worse as time went on.

I'd always been aware of a presence from day one when I moved in there and also before that when the place was being decorated and made ready for business, and the grand opening.

There was this heavy darkness that followed me around the place and at each corner, I decided to go, it was there. To begin with, I didn't think much of it, though as time passed I began to realise this feeling was not good and most definitely not nice. It was creepy and made me feel on edge. Like that type of feeling when you'd be sat with your in-laws around the dinner table, on edge, feeling eyes following you around, especially when you opened your mouth to speak, and then that creepiness of your partner's dad as he perved down on you, hiding behind his glasses, but you'd know exactly what he was thinking. Yeah, well, that feeling. Yuck. So there it was the presence of something or someone within my shop, my new business. Great, just great, I thought, and it was obviously not what I needed.

I would say it all started with a sickness...

CHAPTER NINETEEN

The End is Nigh and the Nigh is Now

And in the end, all I learned was how to be strong alone.

Unknown

Diane

And so it began, the complete and distinct unravelling of it all, in a complete burst of complex and unruly fire, without warning, no exception, and no reasoning behind it, just fury, disdain, and irreparable consequence.

I decided that was it. Well, at least I think I did because I knew for sure there were no options left; there was no hope, no outlook or saviour for me now. I was a lost cause and hope for this earth and I wanted to disappear forever where no one could find me or talk to me ever again.

I wanted peace, silence and calm.

I wanted the control and this may have been the only way to get that - it was what I wanted, needed and deserved – yet I was lost and unsure with nowhere to go.

Who, and just what exactly, had I now become?

I felt it was unfair and sad that I could no longer just be

myself, enjoying what my life should have been and not what it had become. I blamed myself for it but I also blamed him, Daniel. He did nothing to help no matter how hard or how much I begged, cried and asked, pleading with him on all accounts, and yet there was absolutely no interest from him, no attention and no help.

I blamed Daniel; he was the devil.

Emily

My odd relationships during my teenage years were the precursor to the main big and meaningful relationships that I was yet to have, discover, and go through. I'd say my first serious one started off with a young guy, similar in age to me at the time, at 18/19 years old. He was in every way the definition of a bad gut instinct and somewhat not the ideal guy you would entrust and have a loving courtship with. It started off as a chance meeting where we had physically bumped into one another on the street. Of course, I had seen lots of romantic films before and that did not help the situation, leading me to believe that: *wow this is fate, meant to be, you don't just bump into people and start chatting, it must be fated for me, and it was, it was fated all right because it was a lesson in due course and one that I hugely would fail!*

Jamie was a charming young guy, suited and booted type of style with a hint of trendiness and I liked it very much. I'd always envisioned being with someone who was smart, polite and dressed well, someone who was like me, as that was how I liked to be and be seen. Something or someone screamed at me from within, trying with difficulty to tell me that Jamie was not the kind of guy I should continue talking with, never mind meeting. Stupidly, I ignored it, going with my original thoughts that this connection was rare and meant for me due to the way we had met.

The first date was rather odd on my part, we met for drinks in town and I remember feeling uncomfortable. It was a hot summer's evening and I was very thin, all the while having the constant belief that I needed to watch my figure. I picked out what I thought to be a beautiful smart outfit to wear for a first date and what continuously bothered me was that I could not stop this uneasy feeling. I'm not sure if it was due to fear or if it was a prior warning as I hadn't experienced anything quite as bad like it before with anyone else, however, I continued to get ready and travelled by train to Glasgow station. We got chatting over drinks and discovered that we had some common interests. We were both studying at the time, him at university, me at college before I enrolled on the university. We both wanted similar things - to grow up, get good jobs, settle down, get married and have children, and more than likely all in that succession. There must have been things about him that I wasn't too sure of, but I ignored them and replaced those doubts with the good and positive things about Jamie. We said our goodbyes after a short but just okay date.

He arranged to meet me again and I had agreed at the time though I was thinking to myself I would decide later. He messaged me to conclude arrangements for our next date and told me that he'd made the decision to come and pick me up and take me out for dinner, to a luxury steakhouse a good drive away from where we both stayed.

Jamie lived quite a bit over the opposite side of Glasgow from me, which was a blessing. I remember loathing just how far away he stayed and dreaded ever having to actually drive there as it was almost an hour in the car and the only way to get there was via about a hundred motorways. I reluctantly agreed and took my friend's advice that I should at least give him one more chance.

Giving Jamie one more chance was set to be one in the long line of mistakes I would make in this life.

When he arrived at my mother's address where I was living at the time, he was suited and booted again and he seemed very shy and quiet, almost sheepish. We drove off, I was looking forward to our dinner. Upon arriving and being shown to our seats I got the impression that I had already done something wrong, or that he didn't quite approve of it. I wondered if it was something I said, a look I gave him, or how I carried myself, was it even how I laughed?

I still do not know what it was, but there it was, right there. Without me really realising it, he had made me feel uncomfortable.

We chose our dinner options from the provided pre-theatre menu. Jamie chose rare steak which, of course, he would, being a man, and I chose steak too but very well done. I'm not the biggest meat fan, however, I thought I'd give it a try, seeing as he'd brought me here and how expensive it all was. He made comments about my steak and how I'm wasting it by having it blackened to death, all the while looking at his own with blood freshly running from it that made me feel uncontrollably sick, plus how dare he comment on my food choices!

Things were yet to get worse, every time I put my fork to my mouth I could feel him watching me or at least I was thinking that, but all was confirmed when each time I rose my head to look straight at him, there he was indeed watching me eerily, intensely, and almost in a judging way. I found this extremely odd and enough was becoming enough for me at this point. He was still quiet within himself and seemed as if something was troubling him at the back of his mind.

At last, the bill arrived and I thought, *Great I can get out of here and only need to endure the journey home!*

Jamie kindly paid and we set off.

When we got back to the car, he said to me, "I have got you a surprise."

I instantly let out a little, "Oh!" with excitement.

Bear in mind that this was about to become my first and most serious relationship with a guy and I stupidly got carried away with him. He pulled out the biggest bouquet of flowers I had ever seen, they were exquisite. Big yellow sunflowers in amongst the white and orange-toned roses. I couldn't believe it and to top it off he had bought me a huge box of my favourite Thornton's chocolates. *How did he know?*

And just like that I was fixed to him, all over a box of chocolates and a bunch of flowers. I was the easiest pleased female ever!

What a wash, what a fool - and what a con by him.

Jamie, I have to hand it to him, was very attentive in that way and bought lots of lovely feminine goodies to lure a woman in closer, but I was just excited by the things I received from him. I recall on Valentine's Day he lavished me with amazing things like perfume, chocolates, more over-the-top flowers and some CDs. It was unreal. He cooked me a romantic dinner and played a Barry White CD, which was a bit premature for the short amount of time that we'd been seeing one another, though it was sweet and thoughtful.

I still couldn't shake that initial odd feeling I'd had about him though and the long creepy gazes continued. Then the comments he made about every little thing became more and more frequent. We only saw each other once a fortnight on average, due to the nature of our busy student lives of studying and exams, however, when I did see him he always found something to pick on me for.

It would be questions and remarks like:

What are you wearing?

Dressed like an office worker again today?

Or, Not sure your hair looks good like that, take it down.

All these little things would build up in my head subconsciously and this behaviour of his changed the real person I was bit by bit. I'd say even now, today, many years later, I still am not the same girl that met Jamie.

He made sure that he changed that and yes, some may say it's my fault, or I shouldn't have allowed him to do that to me, but as a wise lady once said to me, "It's life experience and you're kidding yourself on if you believe you would've stayed the same as you were at 18 anyway."

Perhaps that is so.

And to cut a very long drawn story of me and Jamie short, it all ended eventually after he accused me of cheating and abused me verbally at all costs.

What topped it off were the constant comments, such as, "If I was ever going to murder anyone, I'd take them out to sea, kill them, then tie a slab of concrete to their feet, and I'd drop them into the middle of the ocean."

What made that even more frightening was his high hopes

of building a boat with his dad, and, wait for it, he actually asked me if would I go sailing with him out to sea! Errr... no thanks!

When we had our final argument in a lone car park while sat in his car, he made it a priority to play with a long piece of rope that he'd looped up then tied into knots while asking me, "What do you think of this? Isn't it amazing how tight a knot you can put in a rope, look how you can pull it together?"

He would then stretch and tug this rope right in front of my face.

Struggling to control the situation or him with his rope, I concluded the conversation, and we left it at that.

He later messaged me with a subtle, "I love you, Emily." However, I would have liked an apology.

Typical, egotistical, man/man child.

After that, many weeks passed and I did not see or hear from Jamie until I began noticing a car similar to his at the time constantly at my back while I was out driving to and from local places. For example, the gym, the shops or even University. It was beyond strange considering how far away he lived and his busy schedule, but I knew for certain that it was him. That extreme and odd behaviour at the age of 18, frightened me and sent a specific and clear message that guys/men were to be watched and dissected until I knew for sure whether they were complete weirdos or not, going forward.

Then the phone calls began, constant, at all hours of the night, particularly at weekends, and prank calls along with texts - it just never ended. I considered it over some time but eventually felt the only way I could stop this was to get the police involved and inform them as to what was going on. They advised me that I should hand in my phone for several weeks so that they could log and keep track of the incoming calls and therefore eventually trace it back to the origin and the person who was sending them. Sadly, I needed my phone for work at the time and I couldn't give up my phone for the process. And that was that, I just had to put up it for the foreseeable future and it continued for a very long time, but as all things do, it came to a final end.

Fast forward to ten years later and he is now recently married to a girl with the exact same first name as myself. Bizarre. However, that doesn't matter, I just hope and pray that he is treating this woman correctly and has changed his awfully strange ways.

CHAPTER TWENTY

Alone

You can't break glass and expect to put it back together again, even if you somehow do, the cracks will forever show.

Unknown

Emily

For as long I could possibly think back or remember, I had always loathed being alone or on my own. 'Within my own company' - or however, people might like to say it - just the very thought of it and the fact of it - I cannot come to grips with.

I find my own company nice at times.

By that, I am merely talking of being alone for say a couple of hours at best. However, to have to spend days, nights or even weekends all on my lonesome, I have never enjoyed or liked that.

I would guess that most people don't as, hey, who actually likes having just themselves to talk to, or even alone within the four walls around you, as they stare at you, closing in on you, stating, '*You're alone, you're alone! Where are your people, your friends, your family, anyone? Hello?*'

I was aware that I did not, or more like could not, fathom living life by myself.

Over the years I've seen it in many, from strangers to people I've known. They had little to no company and found themselves in a situation of being by themselves. They had to learn to take it all with a pinch of salt, though over time they seemed to have found it to be a good thing.

Nope! No way I decided that a lonesome life was not for me.

Consequently, my plan was to find someone nice and have a good, strong, healthy relationship which would first and foremost be my ticket out of the world of being alone.

I truly believed that I needed to be with someone who would make me happy and give me all the comfort I so desperately deserved in this world. The way I viewed things in my overly complex mind and the wonders of imagination were that the world is extremely small and I was rather large within that small circular-shaped object.

I saw in my mind's eye that I was excessive within this realm and that there just weren't endless amounts of people, beings or things out there for my heart to find or desire. Because of that, mindless thoughts and excuses would enter my mind as to how I was ready to accept anything less than human and put it before myself - the first thing that could embrace me with warmth - even if it was fake and untrue.

Looking back, I suppose I did not have many friends in my little world and certainly not any that were fully available with arms wide open offering their ailing support, comfort, trust and dedication to our friendship.

All of these things were amiss in any of the friends I shared my time with and, evidently, I knew there and then I did not have anyone.

I had a family but obstinately that handful-sized amount of family members I'd acquired were not always there when needed at the times the need was the greatest and they possibly didn't make me feel or give me the full extent of the warmth I required.

An overly efforted hug and constant reassurance were what I was looking for, and most likely needed when times get rough.

I can't remember clearly the first time I felt alone and by myself, though I do recall that I knew and pursued my independence from a young age. This reaffirmed my belief that I must create a life for myself with the perfect person by my side at all times, eventually having a giving family. This then would ensure that I would never be a person who lived quietly, rotting away, with not a soul on this planet having known anything about it.

My family and friends all said that I was needy, but I could never imagine or see it like that.

I had a sibling, of course, nephews and nieces too, however, it was not the same as having your own living breathing soul by your side, accomplished and created through the love of your soulmate, a person who would be bound to be by your side for all Eternity.

That's sadly not true reality; it is fiction.

Diane

I hated life as it was – in the Here and Now.

As each day unfolded, I became more exasperated and suffocated by everything and everyone around me.

Life was closing in as I was spending out my life sentence. Grief, discontent and hatred filled me, flowing over me like the darkest of pestilential-filled seas. Although I tried extremely hard, never failing to fight my inner feelings, things just simply got too much.

Daniel was worsening, becoming more and more fraught, he frightened me and I felt dismayed by him. When things were not going his way, he'd take it out on me and little James, which I saw as unfair though I did love Daniel with all my soul and might. I could not let him go and neither could I give up on my love for him. He knew how much I cared and I knew what he had done for us. He would tell me he loved me often enough, however, he would leave us to ourselves equally.

I wanted his presence around at every given moment, considering my deteriorating state and the unpleasant way in which I would handle things.

I was a pot on the stove just tepidly waiting to reach the 'boiling over' point.

We used to do things together as a couple, even as a family, but he would rather leave us - leave me on my own with James - and do 'other' important things, and not be there to help me, his wife, whom he says he appreciates and wants to be with.

I couldn't trust him even though I knew he wouldn't do anything to upset me.

A little more attention, giving and love – that's what I needed the most.

I wanted some acknowledgement and understanding, I wanted to plead with Daniel to never let me go or leave me on my own, just to stay with me and be with me forever.

Once again, I left the house and bought some yellow flowers from the local shop down by the sea. Myself and little James slowly cruised back up the short road to our house and I placed James into his baby bouncer. I took the flowers and arranged them with water in a vase, placing them carefully into the bevelled glass.

As I stared into the glass prolongingly, I would wonder, *What if I was a flower, would I have feelings? Would I grow beautifully? Would I survive in there?*

James would then let out a cry, needing me, needing his mummy to come and rescue him from lying slouched within his bouncer. He needed me very much and I was always there at his beck and call. He was just a little innocent child relying on me for everything, relying on Daniel for nothing. Hours passed and I could not list or speak of what I had done to pass the day.

Daniel would come home a while later, his face full of aggression and toil.

I would ask him, 'What is the matter?' only to be met with a reply of a shrug and a grunt. He went into the kitchen to look at the beautiful golden and yellow tones of the flowers I'd bought earlier. Then he looked displeased, wondering who had purchased them.

Knowing it was myself who'd bought the flowers, I did not see the issue, however, he left me feeling unnerved by his reaction and my thoughts raced as I wondered why he behaved in that way.

The night was finished and we were yet to face each other in the morning.

Daniel was a very well put together and young looking man, despite the fact that he was now fast approaching his 40s. By calling him 'young' I meant that he 'had it together, as people would say. On the outside he appeared normal, as if all was right in his world, and that not much that could floor him. However, I did occasionally surmise that all was not what it seemed with him on the inside.

Scant snippets of his behaviour were what would lead me to this judgemental portrayal.

I loved him dearly as always, and I was still a doctor, yet I could not diagnose or comment on just what was wrong with either of us. Lack of sleep - yes, lack of emotion at times - yes, lack of trust - I considered.

What I really wanted was confirmation that he loved me as much as I did him.

On my 34th birthday I felt extremely groggy and couldn't get up out of bed, I felt as though a bus had driven right through me during the night and I ruminated about what may have caused this unwanted feeling, that continued on for the next day and day after. A few days of relief from it then came, where I felt like myself again, however, I still had the depression and fatigue. Then boom like a tidal wave this time, I was floored again. The days were too meaningless and joyless, they got worse as time passed.

As James grew from baby to toddler, I traversed into a deeper cave of disheartenment.

I took myself off to Lulworth Cove for an afternoon of intervention and reinvention, while Daniel tended to our son for once. I don't recall how I came to arrive there, yet I did and I enjoyed listening to the groaning sound of the tumultuous sea waves, an old-time favourite, a drug to calm my emotional outpour of tears and upset. I believed the waves were trying to tell me something, coercing me into them, pulling like the force of magnetic field energy.

Looking deeply and hypnotically at them, I loathed the waves for their power and strength and all at once I wanted to go right there, right then, into them, and play with their up and down exasperated motions of movement.

I suppose I wanted to get lost.

A twinkle appeared in one eye and sparks of feelings came back to my hands and feet after having a momentary out of body experience, or some sort of psychosis, which I could not tell a soul about, or they would have me off and away for good. I would never see my boys again.

I grabbed my billowing scarf that dangled down longer at one side and my small handbag, and I fled the scene. As I raced past at speed I choked when the sea air caught at the back of my throat and I needed to catch my breath. Falling to my knees and onto the damp sand my eyes gravitated upwards to the edge of the cliff and it looked perfect or at least quiet, undisturbed, time lost, and yet to be desired.

The cliff was inviting me up there to join it, into its beautiful calming warmth that lay within its being.

Time chimed, I knew I must get back, being close to dinner and everything else that was planned out for me that night, with all my chores. Slight happiness overcame me, perhaps the fresh air had done me good or calmed my nerves, though I felt renewed and ready to start the rest of the evening.

Daniel greeted me at the door with a screaming, hysterical and uncontrollable James who he obviously could not cope with. Subsequently my husband hounded me with questions, grilling me about *where I had been, why I was away for so long, what was I thinking in my head leaving him like that.*

Daniel told me to go, it had been his idea, I was sure of it, at least I thought I was sure of it. Maybe he was right, perhaps I hadn't told him, just left him on his own, alone, struggling.

I couldn't even tell my own mind anymore, what was happening to me?

The noise of the ocean and the sights of the crystal blue sun catching waters replayed in my mind, it was instant as if to remind me of its stabilising effects and the way in which it could help to calm me into peace. And then the smashing of glass sounded in the background, severe and intense, as it brought me right back to our home, Daniel showing serious disappointment as his eyes looked into mine.

"How could you, what is wrong with you Diane? You need help I know you do.'

I was standing there with blood streaming down my fingers and looked up at the kitchen window where there were broken shards of glass everywhere, my left eye hurt and had a jagged feel to it. I realised then a large tumbler glass had been broken, thrown, smashed I honestly do not know how, what I did know was that I must have done it.

Me, it must have been me; I don't remember it, but all I can feel right now is pain, fear and worry.

CHAPTER TWENTY ONE

The Main Man

The loss is not material, if it is material.

Sense n Sensical

Emily

And there he was the perfect man in all his glory. Stood right in front of me, yet another chance meeting. At first I didn't even fancy him or remotely feel interested towards him in that way, though something striking soon formed as the conversation between us hit an all-time high and flowed like the Orinoco river.

Our connection was steady and wholesome, with an edge to it in every way.

We had so much in common already and that was just the start of what was to come. Lewis was a couple, almost three years older than I was and I found that attractive in itself as I had always aspired to find someone with apt maturity and a little bit a definition on the frame as opposed to someone my own age, young, undefined and inexperienced. I had been there done that, and worn the t-shirt, now I needed a man. A real man with a good job, oozing prospects and ambition such as myself, and a passion for life, as mine was a little bit flat at the time of our meeting.

Lewis was a councillor, working for the local health board close to where I lived at the time and I was referred to him for a helping hand to deal with my anxieties, worries, and my low mood at coping with a business, the physical pain after my accident, and the general everyday matters.

He was excellent, approachable, professional, intelligent and a great listener.

He took great care in responding to me with the utmost calm and caring manner, which again drew me in. In total, we had together twelve long sessions and for most of them we laughed and chatted carelessly about general things, topics and hobbies we both enjoyed.

Lewis was leading a very similar life to mine at the time, as he shared with me that we drove the same car, he also had a business on the side of his own, and he was also renting his own flat. All these things were exciting and wonderful qualities and I felt that I had never been in a position where I had someone in front of me with such maturity, grace and a tight grip on life. It was refreshing, intriguing and I wanted more.

Of course, we got onto the subject of partners, what with all the chemistry between us, we felt the intense need to know whether either of us was partnered up or not. Lewis told me of a recent love interest who he had taken on some dates and how she eventually gone off him and moved onto someone else. I felt the hurt and sadness for him straight away as he told me the story, he didn't appear too bothered though I could tell the disappointment was still lurking somewhere inside.

There is nothing worse than rejection.

In the end we never discussed my relationship status which was something that held no interest. Lewis knew I liked him. I was discharged and told him I was moving away to another area. The day he let me go, his mood was most definitely off and I felt rather odd in his company. However, there was not much I could do to change that.

Months passed, my life decreased in some ways and gained most certainly in others, and when I had time, I often found my mind wandering back to Lewis. I wondered how he is getting on, where is he now? Did he like me? When I was tidying up one day, I discovered an old letter with his full name in the letter heading. I felt a sense of completion as I just knew what to do next. With the art of social media, I found him and sent him a blunt, friendly message, simply asking if he remembered me. I was sure he would either not reply or reply with something along the lines of 'yes, but I'm with someone'. My heart was constantly sinking while I awaited his reply, and then it came a full day later with a very happy, appreciated response and I had the overwhelming sense of relief and a steadier feeling of completeness come over me once again.

I felt that this was fate.

We had our first date two weeks after from the day when I got in contact with him and we never parted, except for some days while we were both attending our work. The next eight months appeared perfect, full of harmony and bliss. After this period I had met his parents whom he called by their first names Janette, Jan for short, and Colin, both in their 60's and nice enough, perhaps a bit on the quiet side for me though that didn't matter as it wasn't his parents I was dating. Then before I knew it, it appeared all at once that we were moving in together to a beautiful, idyllic, newly built house and we had a baby on the way. Yes, very soon, some would say, but it felt right. Lewis promised me the absolute world.

He promised always to be there, to love me and to give me everything I had ever wanted and so far it was looking so good.

Things truly could not have been better as I lived and breathed each day with such joy, enthusiasm, happiness and control. I felt I had and was in control and just everything was perfectly rosy in my world. From the outside looking in and partly to the future, that world was about to be taken out by a devastating tsunami, or an earth-shattering meteor, or rocked and broken apart by a psychotic tornado. Things were fine and I was doing okay until the problematic symptoms of my pregnancy began to kick in, causing raucous and nauseating pain, frequent hospital trips only to be diagnosed with normal pregnancy symptoms. I wanted badly to feel normal again, to feel alive, and not just alive to be the home for the little soul that was living within me.

I felt myself wrapped up in thoughts that I shouldn't have experienced, such as:

Why did I do this to myself?

Why did we decide to have a baby so soon?

I started to feel as if it were all a bit too soon and that we should have waited, but then I would feel an internal flutter or a kick or some kind of movement from the tiny human growing inside of me and it brought me back to some sense of reality that this was a very real situation and that I had to enjoy it, if not go along with it for now, for my unborn baby's sake. All I wanted and needed was to feel untimely normal to some extent and just to feel like me again.

I felt out of control though all the while somewhere within I relished the fact that I was carrying a beautiful life inside of me, a fate that not many can have or achieve easily.

Following on from that, I found myself coming across many women who in fact could not conceive easily, now there it was - striking me like a hundred bricks all at once - the ultimate guilt. Even my baby flipped a little inside my tummy as he/she could feel the emotions that I was experiencing right there and then, and just exactly what I thought about me being pregnant. There was this wonderful woman stood in front of us, telling us she may never get the chance or opportunity to experience life's best joy, and that is to be a mother.

The pregnancy became increasingly worse and I hated to admit it but I began to feel as though if there had been an option for it to be over at that moment, I would have taken it. I had the odd scare and landed up in hospital on a couple of partly dreaded occasions. I would pray that they would say I needed to give birth early and that the baby would do the rest of the cooking in the hospital incubator.

I'd truly like to hope I'm not the only woman to ever have thought this. I suppose it was a mixture of severe fear and anxiety about the pain becoming worse, my walking abilities crushed further, and my relationship already suffering massively as it took more blows to the point of no return. I felt I was at the point of no return, I would and could never surely be me again, or have my body the way I had it before. When the hospital gave me the news that all was okay and to try to relax, I was relieved yet disappointed altogether. When I discovered I was having a daughter, I felt relieved that she was well and happy, developing as she should be. However, I had always had a sharp inclination that it was a boy I was carrying, a little son, and when I was told it was a girl my heart sank slowly and just a small amount as if I had allowed it to sink any further, it wouldn't have survived enough to come back up. I supposed I had it so well planned out in my head and in my belief that she was a he and that my first born would be my son, yet life surprises you every day. I then had to develop and grow a loving bond towards my first unborn child now a female, a little girl, and I began to realise that there was no changing that fact now that it was set in stone and I was going to give birth to a daughter.

I did, I gave birth to a healthy, bouncy, beautiful baby girl, weighing a great 8 and a half pounds and she was the best baby.

I, on the other hand, was the worst new mum there could be. I had seen the whole process as a job or even a chore, instantly applying all of my perfectionism OCD overtaking issues into my new job as a mother, which led me down a darkened, murky, garden path and a slippery slope to the art of not being able to cope at life, or at anything. And because I then became intolerably impertinent, I also pushed away Lewis. My other half, the love of my life, my world, my pick me up everything that I thought I had, he was gone in an instantaneous jolt, a switch going off from light to dark.

A true happiness changed to an unforgivable sadness.

Lewis resented me, he changed, I changed, we grew apart when we should have been growing together, loving together, and raising our beautiful little child. Instead we took the train of deportation further and further away from each other and it turned into the world's worst relationship.

His distance, the long glares of disgust and lost hope arose, without the imagination of how we might piece our marriage back together again.

Meetings at work became a reality and late home arrivals became the norm. I was left at home with a never-ending crying newborn, and I resolved to believe that I could no longer do it. No longer did I wish to be a mother, a partner, a business owner. Nothing, everything, just disintegrating right before my eyes. Lewis tried, I must admit, but I pushed him away. The more I pushed, the more he bit, the more he fought not for me but with me and against me.

My husband turned on me like a dog that had taken one too many knocks.

Lewis Mackinnon

I loved Emily, I really did and I still do, but by God, it was hard work.

All I had ever wanted for my life was to work hard, earn for my family. Be a husband, a father and a family man. I had done everything for them, more than any other man would, and what had I got for it? Nothing but constant judging, groaning, despising and full body loathing. If only I could have made her see, made her understand.

I thought it was too late when I realised that Emily had started to hate me and, if I'm being truthfully honest, I didn't like her very much either at that point.

The stress felt all too much and other things were getting into my mind where I couldn't stop nor prevent the consequences if I continued on that way. I hoped that she would never know or discover that, as it was not my fault, it was not me. I loved our child so very much, yet she told me I did not and most days she would say that I was not good enough, not the father she dreamed of for her daughter. I thought then that she had issues, from the birth - possibly post-natal issues. I'm not a doctor, all I knew was that we could not continue on like that.

I am Lewis and I am just a normal man.

When I met Emily I never expected any of it to end up like what it became. I did everything imaginable for her, for our daughter. From nothing to something, I'd built a life for my wife and child and this was the thanks I received. I'd worked extremely hard to make ends meet, to provide them with a happy stable life, but it was always returned to me like a slap in the face, sometimes quite literally. For instance when Emily was annoyed with me and believed in her head, her own little world, that I had been cheating or lying, or keeping things from her. Maybe I was, maybe I had to, I had no choice but to keep some things from her that might cause pain and hurt, or worry for her, she had enough to deal with.

The main fact was I felt that I could not do right for doing wrong, and it was the feeling that I lived with every single day of the marriage.

How much longer could we actually live in that negative, dreary state, with no positive outlook?

I felt genuinely trapped by her at times and I was so isolated, I had no one to turn to except my parents. However, I didn't wish or want them to know what was really going on, or anyone else to know for that matter. Some things were truly best kept behind closed doors. And a door it was, the last time Emily closed the door on us and the beautiful loving home I had built and given her - for us, for our family, she let it burn to the ground.

Emily destroyed every single trace, each living memory we shared, gone in the flames.

I blamed her for all of it.

Emily

Loss is a funny old thing, funny not the comical sense, but more the odd and unexpected, strange, if you like, kind of sense.

One where I cannot put my finger on it or contemplate exactly why or how it happens.

One thing I do know for sure, however, is that I have suffered great loss in my short life, perhaps not by death but I have lost the living; every living thing I once had or owned all gone without a trace, a shadow left behind, a second thought to ponder on just exactly what I had. So many regrets, so little time, how I wish at times I could go back and fix it all, start again. I question myself.

Would it be any different this time?

Would it change?

Most importantly, would I be happier?

Because I was not a happy person. So many things around me had caved in or grown tighter, it had become harder to breathe, harder to exist in this ball of what was once my life. After I had given birth to my beautiful daughter Ava May, still in shock and wonder about why she was a girl and not the son I had dreamt of, or always imagined from when I was young. The son I had been followed by in mind, body and spirit, like I could feel his very presence and I had known that he was mine, yet there she was, a daughter, looking up at me.

I had to face facts and accept that this was my fate.

After Ava-May was born, my world began to spiral and was torn apart as I suddenly experienced panic, trauma and stress all at once. Lewis only contributed to that, with his distant looks, shallow emotion, and pity on what I had become. I needed him then more than ever, his love, his warmth, his comfort and his help, yet it was absent. None of what I believed I needed from him was available and I found myself in a very lonely place.

As things eventually progressed, I found myself fantasising regularly about death and about ending it.

The pain, the anxiety, the suffering.

My life to me was one big misery, even my beautiful baby could not pull a smile onto my face. I knew Lewis and I were lost now and there wasn't much hope for reuniting us back, despite him promising endlessly to me that he would always be there, he would never go, never leave and yet he did. On more than one occasion after a minor disagreement and all the while he knew how much I was suffering after Ava-May was born as one ailment lead to another, all stemming from the difficult birth which I had endured to bring her into this world.

Lewis left me, left us, just for a few days while he stayed at his parents' home. Jannette and Colin were both in their 60's and yet neither had any common sense when it came to this entire situation. I begged them, pleaded with them for help many a time and yet no help they gave me or offered to me. Instead they harboured that 'piece of shit', as I thought of my husband at the time, in their home and fed, watered, and provided him with fresh towels and linen.

The rage that unfurled within me caused me to lose touch with everything.

The fantasy I lived on a daily basis was about just how it would feel not to be here anymore, experiencing this devastation, living a lie, in that unhappy, more like miserable, existence.

I felt dead already.

Dead inside, empty, hollow with no more now to offer.

At my lowest depths, I considered just exactly how I would do it. The blast of the train as it derailed by and crashed into me, gone in seconds, left unrecognisable, but at least it would be over. On other days, I would casually graze down to the woodland nearby our house, as I walked slowly, I would be drawn by the trees, their strength and stature. All sorts of images came furiously into my head, almost as if hounding me to actually do what I could envision. I could see rope and ladders and I ran through it in my mind as to how I could possibly get up there, it was another way to be gone, end it all, and for it all to be over with.

STOP, just STOP.

I had to control it and bring my head back around to normality as this was not normal thinking and, deep down, I knew I couldn't really ever go ahead with it; well not yet anyway, however, I took enjoyment in exploring my options. I knew I should really go to see someone for some kind of help yet I was scared and felt alone, at odds with my mind and my feelings and I didn't want to get taken away from my husband or Ava May. I was attached to them as much as they were to me.

In January 2018, I lost my business.

An end of an era, though not to me, not in my head. My head translated to me that it was a loss I would never recoup from, never regain any positive feelings about it, or toward it. And it was all because of him, because of Lewis. He'd expressed continuous concerns over my ability to cope, to function, to run a home, a business, a relationship and cope with a new baby. Really the business didn't fit in, he wanted to be Number One always. So, he talked me into selling it. Knowing I wasn't in the right state of mind and, yeah, perhaps he was right to say that, but to let your partner give up a business that she had spent years on making into a success and having watched it grow, for her to just walk away, that was harsh. I would add that not in any way shape or form was I any better off financially from it. I then resented him forever for this.

In one day, I had lost my business, my self-esteem, my mental control and, most upsetting, I lost my husband too.

I could not fathom just how someone I loved so much could do that to me.

Then came the blame on my part, I blamed myself, I blamed my pregnancy, my birth even my child, my new baby, I told myself over and over that if it wasn't for me and all my problems, I would have managed and I could have done it all, could have been the woman he wanted and needed me to be. I would have made him proud. It is my fault I know it is.

As if all of that was not enough on the surface, deeper down lurked something far worse in the waiting.

Fate? Who honestly knows.

If there is a God or Destiny, just maybe this is the reason why, but at the time you succumb to the every why possible as you try to find the answer and it's like trying to get back out of the vastly sinking sand you have suddenly found yourself in.

It had been a normal day like any other, except it wasn't. Life was not normal for us and it hadn't been for a very long time now.

Lewis went off to work and I was at home with our little Ava-May then eighteen months old. When instead of choosing to go for a nap, I once again made a wrong turn that became a life-changing decision. Most definitely not intentional, however, that didn't matter, it didn't even come into consideration as once the damage was done, it was done, in his book - if not also mine.

I caused a fire within our own home.

What started out as making a simple bit of toast for brunch turned into a full overturning house fire with endless irreparable damage and long-lasting PTSD for the best part. Within seconds of placing two slices of toast into our fairly new, modern white toaster and pushing down the lever, I took my eye off it for mere seconds to check on Ava and as I returned to the kitchen, I glanced into the room. Initially I wasn't appeased to see the smoke and the five centimetre tall, dull orange coloured flames, as they crept upwards from the toaster. I instantly assumed that a crumb was the reason from inside the toaster, perhaps it had caught too much heat and began to smoke. I wafted the toaster back and forth, side to side in the hope that the flames and the smoke would dissipate. To my relief they did, though momentarily only, for the flames came back with a vengeance and grew at an even quicker pace and looking angrier. I could not stop the fire; it was an impossible fight at that moment so I phoned 999 and was advised to take Ava with me and that I should leave the house immediately. Within ten to twelve minutes, two fire engines and nine firefighters had arrived on the scene, to be greeted with the intense, thick, black smoke that threw the large, well-built men backwards.

I was unsure if they weren't expecting the fire to be as bad as it was, but surely with their expertise, any fire would be unpredictable?

The fire was extinguished, everyone was safe. The house was gone. The entire kitchen was gone. Every lick of paint, the almond white coloured walls, all devastated now with thick black soot in and on every wall, every crevice.

The house was unrecognisable and now uninhabitable.

Each memory, each moment, each item in that house, the parts of mine, Lewis', and now Ava May's, life together had been taken from us, destroyed, never coming back, it was over. It was lost; there wasn't anything that anyone could do about it. My fault; even Lewis was sure to tell me that I had caused it and the look in his eye was everything I needed to know.

I wanted to be taken away, relieved and renewed in that sad, unbearable moment.

I wanted to be unknown anywhere and to everyone.

To be free and to start again, not to be tarnished with this brush of horror that I had caused a devastating fire in my very own home.

CHAPTER TWENTY TWO

The End

In the end, there is no end.

Robert Lowell

Diane

I looked up and then down. Never side to side, and most importantly, I did not look back, and that was it, I was gone.

There was no going back, no second chance, no hope, no life; it was all taken from me in that moment.

It was Autumn, my favourite time of the year had just begun to stamp itself on the year, with the slightly windier weather, yet still a touch of warmth in the outdoor temperature. It felt nice. 'Nice' is a poor word as, actually, it felt glorious, just the way I liked it - not too hot, not too cold, not too windy - just right. On hearing the voice inside my own head read out that description of the day's weather, I thought it sounded like something out of 'Goldilocks and the Three Bears' children's story. I should know, as I read it to little James. That's right, James.

When would I ever put him first - at the real forefront of my mind?

I was not completely incompetent, I did love him, except I did not know how to, not properly, and certainly, not good enough. That's definitely not a mother's kind of thing to say and do, yet it was true as I was so far from being the mother I should have been for my son that it cut me up inside.

My heart would clench, I would feel the swishing blood coursing in and out, in a race to keep me surviving this horrid affair that I called 'life'; my life as it was at that time.

I had made it this far and James was now six years old. Still tender enough to be hurt, broken, and for all his dreams and hopes to be dashed, all because of me.

His mother, his strength, his armour, his world.

I had taken that from him, in a blink, in a breath, in a sigh, in a small devastation, yet quickly and fiercely, hopeful yet destroyed. I had done it and there was no going back. My death would be the end, the end of the pain, the end of that year, the end of my life - of his life, James' life, as he knew it.

Would he survive whatever would happen next? Could, or would, he overcome this? Who knew?

It was far too late for me to know anyway.

Six Months Earlier
Daniel Murrison

I could not stand that bitch for one second longer. I wished that she knew the hate I had inside for her, how sick of her I felt. Sick of the life she had given us. No get up and go, no push, no drive.

Nothing... She was Nothing.

I've been living with what I could only describe as *'a box'*, and an empty one at that. She was lacking in love, lustre, and any kind of compassion necessary to be a decent mother, wife or doctor. She was finished in everyone's eyes and there was nothing I could do to help her, not anymore. I still loved her though probably not in the way that I should have and, worst of all, I was not entirely sure or confident in the knowledge that I would be fit enough for young James. He needed a father figure around; he was a boy after all and with an already flailing mother like her, God help him if I turned out to be unable to sustain the life any longer, giving him the help that he needed to survive.

Each night of the week had become the same, day in, day out. I would arrive home from work, late, of course I did, as I could not bear the thought of returning home to the sheer misery on the table, even if I'd been lucky and she had made a decent meal for us, or perhaps even fixed a drink up. You'd think that by now things would be different as the years had passed, but no, still the same.

Perhaps it was my fault - I thought that sometimes when I lay awake at night and I would think long and hard about my actions.

Did I push her?

Push her into things she did not desire, nor want, or need?

Well, if that was actually the case, I would say to her:

'I am truly sorry Diane for my part in the tragedies that came to unfold. Unfold you and unfold us as a family. I honestly did not mean for any of it.

I needed you to be a little calmer, a little quieter, and I had to do what it took to achieve that; I tried my God damned hardest.

I tried with James, to show him what at least one loving parent looks like.

Despite everything you have done, become, and are, he would always pick you over me. Always. You are his mother but he deserves better, you know this, right?

You, I do try to pick you up when you're down, mentally, physically, emotionally, but it is difficult to do when most days you are withdrawn and irresponsibly incoherent.

I just wish we could go back, do things differently, change each other, our ways, bad ways, bad habits, and be better, or at least the way we should have been. Perhaps then things might have been different. Perhaps then we might have just made it.'

Two Months Earlier
Diane

Everything looked to be reaching a boiling point in my life. I literally could not function. I felt weak, lacking in all physical strength and coordination; I hoped it was not another pregnancy.

How would I have coped with that, when I had struggled so much?

Things were extremely rocky and on edge with Daniel, I simply could not bear the possibility of putting myself or my family through that again. The sickness I would feel and the aches, coupled with, my overwhelming lack of feeling inside

— made me wonder how would I be able to cope if it was a pregnancy.

Unsure if I even had the guts to do a test, just to see?

I was a doctor, for Christ's sake! You would think I'd just know if I was pregnant again. Plus the obvious fact that I had been through it once before.

Him – Oh, how would I tell him, if I were indeed expecting again, with him, Daniel?

Part of me was deeply aware that my husband wouldn't be best pleased or remotely interested. He could barely deal with James and he dealt with me in ways he shouldn't, but I knew that I did not give him much choice and that was what I told myself anyway.

However, how could I cope with another one - another child coming into this world that we were living in, this family that we had, this lie that we were living? Was any of this my fault - I knew some things were not right and had not been since the last time I got pregnant, but why do I feel this way?

Why did I struggle in silence?

Why couldn't I change it, or do something to feel better?

Leaving Daniel and James would be sinned upon, my community would never accept that, my church would never forgive. I would have no family to turn to, no friends to call upon, not that I had many left now anyway, thanks to him always painting me in such a darkened light. There were no options. Nothing now. I just wished it could change or be better, I really did, for young James' sake at least.

I would have to take that test; I had to know one way or the other, and once I knew I could cautiously devise upon my options, even if there would not be any.

The Last Day
Diane

I woke early, got up from bed and decided to get dressed. I decided that 'today is a new day, a good day'. I was going to make a new start, whatever that new start was going to be. I picked a white and yellow floral smock top that fell to just below the thighs along with a beige stone coloured pair of wide-legged trousers and some white flat shoes. Feeling bright and sunny, I even looked the part. I continued on to get James up from bed, I helped look out his clothes and prepared breakfast for him, he was looking smart. It appeared to be a lovely day and a day that would transpire well, for once. Daniel was the last to get up. When he did, I had already made him breakfast and laid out some clothes for him and he was pleased with me which made me smile. In that moment I felt happy again, loved, and worthy.

I had come to terms with fact that my period was now well over a month and a bit late and it was about time that I took that test and looked out to the future.

I had picked up a test from the pharmacy earlier in the week and I had been psyching myself up to actually use it and reveal the outcome. Daniel knew nothing of this and I made it my goal to keep it a secret until I knew for sure, then I would make him happy and feel assured that things were going to be different this time around for him and for us as a family.

I left Daniel and James having a father and son chat while I took myself off to the family bathroom. I took the test out of the paper bag, then out of its box, before carefully reading the instructions. I needed to get this right first time around. I did as the leaflet said, placing the now used test up on a flat surface and waited for the allotted time.

Just as I was crumpling up all traces of what I had been doing in there, Daniel knocked on the door, "Diane, what are you doing in there?"

"Shit", I whimpered under my breath, praying he hadn't heard, then I softly replied, "Erm… nothing, love, just the toilet. Why? Is everything okay?"

"Yes, just I wondered, well me and James wondered, if you fancy coming up to the cliff tops for a picnic? Just say yes, James will be disappointed if you don't?"

"Of course," I replied.

I wanted to go, why wouldn't I? It was a nice day; a good day, and I was certainly dressed for the occasion. I felt like today I could breathe once more and I was ready to face a day in the outdoors. Daniel proceeded to tell me to hurry up and in a frantic fashion he made it seem as if we had to rush out of the door. I scrambled to get myself together and, in that moment, realised the test was still not quite ready. Damn it, I would have to leave it until I returned home after the walk and picnic. I assured myself it would be fine as I placed the test carefully into the only cupboard in the bathroom along with its packaging that was not crushed into the original paper bag from the chemist.

I dashed from the toilet and into the bedroom where I fixed my hair a little and grabbed a cardigan. As I did so I noticed that one of Daniel's work shirts was lying in a heap, stuffed to the back of the wardrobe. I probably would not have noticed this usually as I allowed him to get on with the rather unmanly chore of doing the washing and he did insist after all.

However, what had caught my attention was the silver light in my eye from one of his cufflinks that was still attached to the shirt. I noticed it because it was the ones I had bought him for our first anniversary. They were silver with a faint design etched into them and he only ever wore them on a special occasion, such as rare ones when we would go out together which I could actually count on one hand.

Yet this shirt had been freshly worn not too long ago, as I could still smell the cologne emanating from it, albeit now rather musty as it had been stuck into a small space for a while. I pulled it out to have a look and reminisce over the cufflinks and to smell his cologne as it was one of my favourites. It was almost as if he had chosen this recently and especially for me on request, yet we did not enjoy that special night or occasion together. I was taking the shirt away from my face and loosening my hold, when I noticed a red stain, more of a lipstick stain, near the collar and again near the front buttoned area of the shirt. Instantly, I thought and blamed myself for the mishap, as I had just rubbed the shirt in my face for the past few seconds, however, it quickly dawned on me that I did not have any lipstick on that particular day, not yet, as I hadn't gotten around to putting some on my lips. Even if I had done, it certainly would not have been the bright red that I saw on his shirt. Probably more of a light brown, blush colour that I would have chosen.

My head spiralled, my body sank into itself, my blood ran cold, my hands turned sweat infested and I began to feel faint.

The lipstick on his shirt - on my Daniel's shirt - was not mine because it did not belong to me, it belonged to someone else.

Some other woman's lipstick had made the stain on my husband's shirt.

It was too easy to conclude that he was evidently seeing another woman behind my back, after everything, after all we'd been through, what we had become, and what I hoped and tried to achieve each day, a new start, a fresh beginning, a new light – it was all gone in seconds.

I had already died and the reason, the truth was, it was my own fault. I had abandoned him, I wasn't good enough, strong enough, I just was not enough. How could he have done this to me? Easily, came the answer. I had given him no other options. It was as if he was getting the love and happiness he needed at home somewhere else. So many made up events, moments and mini videos started to play off in my head.

Could you imagine going blind for just a moment and you cannot see what is in front of you, yet you can see so many things that you've never ever seen before?

Such as Daniel and his other woman, romancing each other, while I sat at home, crying and depressed. Then him returning home to me, disgusted at the state of me, when he should be disgusted at himself, but he's not, he's disgusted with me, at me, can't stand me, so much so he chose to turn his attention elsewhere.

AND STOP.

What took me out of that temporary blindness and back to reality, was the thud of Daniel's size twelve feet traipsing out of the bathroom. Yes, that's right the bathroom, our bathroom, where I had just used a pregnancy test, of all things. Waiting to see if we were on course to have another child, another one of his children.

I could never look at him again. How could he look at me?

Does he know I might be pregnant? Did he see the test? What does he think?

Does he know I know about the other woman? Does he know I've just seen the shirt? Did he see me in the bedroom holding it?

I wish I could have seen him, then I would've known if he knew. I put the shirt back and closed the wardrobe door, then walked out of the bedroom and shut the door behind me, as if putting a very tight lid on what I'd just witnessed and confronted. My head extremely flustered and not held together whatsoever.

"James", I called, loudly and highly pitched, "Daniel, are we ready to go?"

The reply was a dullened, "Yes," from mainly Daniel, which confirmed my suspicions.

I didn't even have time to check the test. I didn't even want to.

Why would I want to know that I was pregnant a second time to a disgraced cheat - to a man that could do that to me? Why would he even want to be the father of another one of our children when he has a piece on the side, his other woman? He doesn't need me anymore; he certainly doesn't need another baby from me.

Why was he even still here?

What did he want?

His cake? And to eat it, too?

I had to let my thoughts temporarily flow and somewhat run away with me until I got there. Until I got to my special place. Up on the cliff tops, the Dorset cliffs. I could be anyone, be anything, up there. I could do this. We made our way up there, right up to the very top where we could see ahead for miles, the sky was clear, the sight beautiful, capturing and mesmerising. With our picnic in hand and our son James simply delighted to be in our company and for us not to be arguing or disagreeing, it must have felt wonderful for our son.

Daniel looked across to me piercingly, or at least I projected on him that he was looking at me in that way, asked, "What would you like to eat?"

I replied bluntly, "Anything."

I didn't have the guts to talk to him, even if it was only small talk.

James sat on the chequered blanket that we had laid perfectly on the grass-covered cliff top, his legs crossed and a book in one hand, his luscious blonde locks blowing softly in the gentle breeze.

I got lost in his light as it shone all around him, so bright, so loving, there he was my son, my boy, he was doing just fine.

I did love him so very much. Blissfully unaware of his mother and father's difficult demise and what we were all about to face, he should have been allowed to relax and stay wrapped safe and secure in that moment, that look so precious and so perfect.

"Can we take a little walk, love?' asked Daniel, in a summoning tone.

"Yeah, I suppose,' I replied, wistfully, then checked if James would be alright, as I always did.

My head spiralled once again, detailing the ins and outs of why exactly he wanted to walk about and with just me, on our own. I worried, I panicked, I wilted in the cushioning warmth. I couldn't look and I certainly did not want to hear.

My legs turned to jelly as my heart sank, my head told me over and over and over that, '*Today was not a good day, today was not a new start, today was done, it was all done and always was, nothing is good or right and nothing is worth fighting for, nothing, and no one is worth this anymore.*'

It was as if I had completely forgotten all about James, as if he never mattered or existed in my thoughts, in my heart. Selfish, self-loathing, head dictating and torturing to one's self, degrading myself in seconds in every way imaginable. Daniel knew, he knew everything that was obvious, his eyes, his look said it all. His grip was tense and locking, his heart didn't pound not like mine did, he didn't care, he never cared.

I looked out to the sea, swishing back and forth, up and down, wave by wave, white and blue all around. Seagulls slowly gliding by, carried by the wind, faint laughter, children playing, families enjoying every minute and every moment, and mine were fading faster than I could control.

I did not even have time to look back, to say goodbye, to second guess myself, or to check if it was what I really wanted; at no point did I hesitate, even to think that it was all over.

As my first foot crossed over the edge followed by the second, my arms followed, held up high as if I was reaching for one last chance at life, for what mattered, to try to hold on.

My body fell gracefully, my blonde curled locks bouncing swiftly against my cheeks, up and down.

It's true what they say, life really does flash in front of you, right before your last second is up.

My mother and father, my childhood home, my love of Dorset beach and cliffs, the sand, the sea, and Daniel, meeting him, our wedding. Our son James and then I heard it, the scream from above, it brought me out of that flash.

"Muuuuum..?"

I heard it, the last thing I heard, the last ever word, my name, his name for me. My baby, my boy, my James, devastated, shouting after his Mummy, his world, his life, his everything, flashing before him, as I plummeted furiously towards the ground.

My last stop forever.

It wasn't the ground, it was sand, lots of thick, hard, golden crystallised sand, and it would be the harsh impact of my body hitting that which would kill me, ending it all. The thing I had fantasised most about and for so long, never fully believing that I would be brave enough to go through with it.

Everyone would know then how I was, how I felt.

Yet, no one would know the reason, the truth behind it. I could not stop it; I did not try. I never thought this day would arrive as deep down I never wanted it to. However, it has and it has been taken out of my hands and quite literally at that.

If there should be another life, an afterlife after this - I cannot live, I know I cannot live, I will not live through it, I will not rest.

How can I, knowing my young James was on his own, left without his mummy?

We would never be together again.

I was gone, I could not rest with this, not in peace, not with my story untold and with the truth buried with me.

I would always love James.

This other child I was graced with, before we met our end, perhaps we will be born again - both of us - into a new world. One that would treat us right, treat us well. One where we could be happy.

Regardless of any of that for now, I still could not rest, I would not rest.

Someone, somewhere needs to know.

They need to know what he did.

CHAPTER TWENTY THREE

Falling

But it is a curse and a blessing to remember the past, and to know there's a future.

Charlie

Emily

The following weeks were filled with self-contempt and blame, verbal blame, hatred, and what seemed like never-ending upset, destruction, and the feeling of having to rebuild parts of a life that I had only short-lived. It was a relief when it was discovered that I was not to blame for the fire.

There had been an electrical fault within the toaster.

A tightly released breath, a gasp even, abruptly came from my weakened and restrained lungs. The last few weeks had been most difficult and certainly ones to remember. Or at least I would not forget what happened in a hurry that's for sure, however, what I did not realise was that this whole sequence of events had left me with fear, doubt, anguish and anger, as well as the fact that I no longer trusted myself or my husband.

Lewis punished me for it all, he made it evidently clear that he opposed me and was heartfelt that I was to be held responsible for this incident, for all of what happened.

How could he?! How could I?! How could either of us actually fall for this unthinkable horror that he tried to put upon me.

Lewis would say repeatedly that what he was coming away with was it was not true, that he was just upset, however, for me, that was just not good enough. He might have had better luck pissing in the wind. At that time, for me, that represented the frail parts of an already weakened glass box that was beginning to crumble. To put it bluntly, it was the uttermost last thing I needed at that moment in time. The fire was indeed hard enough to deal with, though the total events that were yet to come, were unpredictable, and I was certainly not ready for what I was about to face.

Due to the unforgivable and devastating house fire, that I and my sweet Ava May had suffered the traumatic experience of, we then had to endure the next instalments of this sick, twisted journey of events, as they were about to clatter upon us.

We may have done better if we'd survived a hurricane or tornado, even an earthquake.

I thought that none of those unexplained, unpredictable, weather extremities would have had a molecule's worth of an effect, compared to what we actually went through. When I said we, I meant me and Ava, because we faced it alone, just her and I, together. He was not there.

Lewis caused much grief, problems, which only extenuated into further demise for us all as a family. Looking back, I believe he was struggling in his job, putting endless pressure on himself, along with his other issues that I came to find out later. The day of the fire brought change and major change at that. We were told by the fire crew we would have to find somewhere else to stay for that night and potentially even up to the length of six months. It was a shock. Already still high on adrenaline from saving myself and my baby daughter from a fire that could have been fatal, I pulled myself together and took it all in my stride. I tried hard to get my family through this torrid time as best we could.

We went to a hotel room which was alright though rather cramped, so we then moved to a bigger room there. Packing up our small quantity of belongings felt tedious, long drawn out and very tiring, as it pressed onto our useless time.

That's right, we felt completely useless, what could we do?

Stuck there in those hotel rooms, they were not a patch on our beautiful home. Suddenly, so many pictures came furiously into my head and I began recalling each thing that happened during our time in that very home.

I must have been extremely far away from reality as I had not remembered much while I was actually living in it, other than a constant heaviness, as if someone was preying upon my soul, trying to destroy me and everything I had worked for.

My relationship with Lewis was very much already broken, despite the overture times when I tried to repair the damage and make the way he treated me work. It did not. I recalled always telling Lewis I just needed out of that house; it was beautiful in decoration, in design, but something there was just not right from the day we had moved in. I hadn't experienced much in the spiritual sense, not since the photography business, and especially not since I asked for all of those 'experiences' so to speak to just stop. However, I had a fair few odd times in the home when I experienced things that for some would be extremely worrying and frightening.

However, I just felt that it was more of a warning rather than anything else.

It began one night when Ava May was only a few months old and still in our bedroom in her cot at the end of our king-size bed. I awoke one night to find a man standing at the bottom of the bedroom, peering over Ava's cot and then looking up towards Lewis and I. It took me aback as I gathered myself together trying to understand who this person could be and what was he doing in our room.

Two or so weeks prior to this, on many of my walks outdoors with Ava, we would stroll around the whole of the new build estate with its 900 houses. It had been built on previously used grounds, some parts of the old buildings had been kept and renovated into flats. These particular structures had belonged to a demolished mental hospital that was still running around up until thirty years ago. It gave me an eery feeling I must admit, although the estate was stunning, populated with many families and young working couples. It was not the type of place to live and grumble at.

It was pure privilege to live there.

The houses ranged from flats to oversized, underfilled miniature mansions, with their sale tags for well over half a million pounds.

As Ava and I passed by, Ava in her pram of course, I would use the gleeful walking time to enjoy looking in depth at other people's houses and their streets, and always wondered for a couple of seconds just who exactly lived in a house like that. Something that caught my attention on multiple occasions while out on our daily walks were the street names. They all were called after something or most likely someone, and the one that stood out most for me, for reasons unknown at that time other than I just felt warmly drawn into it, was the street name of 'Rutherford Drive'.

I thought it to be rather unusual to name a street after that name and began my quest while pacing along, my mind ticking over time, as always, pondering, mentally investigating why it would be called that. I came to the conclusion in my head that it must be named after someone and I left the thought of it at that.

When I saw this man in our room that particular night, Ava was not well and she had been suffering from a seasonal cold. She was a little under the weather, however, it was under control and well managed. The man stood with glasses covering his face and appeared most interested in what he was studying or looking at, then it dawned on me his attire was peculiar and different to the norm. He wore a long white doctor's coat and it was from an era that was apparent to me as from many decades ago.

As quick as I had seen him and watched him, he had also noticed my interest as I gazed across at him, and he disappeared gently into thin air.

Not long afterwards, even with the unsure feeling I had in my body, I quickly drifted back into a deep sleep and awoke the following morning to find Lewis and Ava May both gone, although I could hear them downstairs giggling away as they organised breakfast.

I took that time to do a little investigating into what I had witnessed that night, as it was fresh in my mind as I had now awoken properly. My first and obvious opinion was that as this was built on some old hospital grounds and the man in my room looked like a doctor of some sort from his attire, I felt perhaps he was from that place but in another time period. I typed into the search engine on my phone internet to find pictures of doctors at the hospital.

One stood out clear as day. I immediately recognised him. It was that of a Dr James Rutherford. He had been the top psychiatric doctor at the hospital that my estate was now built on.

Instantly, chills and shivers ran up and down my spine, then it hit me brazenly once again as I remembered the name of that street I had noticed while out walking, Rutherford Drive. To my astonishment the street was indeed named after this doctor in the photo, Dr James Rutherford. The very man I had seen in our bedroom last night.

It all made sense as to who he was and why I had noticed the street beforehand, but I was haunted now by questions about him.

Why was this doctor in our bedroom?

Why was he peering or checking over each of us?

It left an unexplained, emptiness within. I had no choice then but to get up, move on from it, and to enjoy the rest of my day, with the hope that the doctor would not return. What left me even more astounded was what happened towards the end of that week when we all became very unwell, needing rest and recuperation.

Perhaps he was there as a warning? Or to look after us?

What if it was something more sinister?

It could be the reason why I knew for sure I needed out of that house.

I needed out of it all, if I could have taken a drug to block it out, I would have, I could have, but all I had to literally block things out were my dreams. Yet again, the overwhelming dreams and conjuring of the night's eye took over me, whether it was stronger than the form of any alcohol or drug was disputable. My dreams succumbed me into their darkness and also into their light, as they carried me to the place I needed to go just as much.

I felt safe there, I wanted to sleep forever, an escape, a saviour, another realm where I felt I could be happy, be safe and be me.

Nothing mattered, no one mattered or cared, neither did I care about them, it was the perfect harmonious bliss that I needed more than anything at that given time, because in reality I was struggling. I was suffering, failing at the hands of life, and what was a relationship of marriage, of motherhood, of everything, as it would seem at the time. However, it was not, it was complete destruction, devastation, and a total waste of everyone's time, including my own.

Although it was not a dream, it was my reality, I could not get Dr James out of my mind and the pondering thoughts of the reason why he had come to me, to us.

A week or perhaps even two had now passed since that visit from the doctor to our home and within days of just that, we were all struck down with a terrible cold, each one of us coughing and spluttering, grasping our chests, even little Ava May. I came to the conclusion the doctor had come to forewarn me of such illness and that had put my mind back at gentle ease, until another couple of weeks on top of the visit to the illness, we had, or I really should say I had, the devastating fire.

Could the reason behind the ghostly doctor's visit have been a forewarning of the fire?

Or was there more to come?

Each move from our home, to hotel, to another home and another again, when finally we settled into a quaint cottage somewhere out in the rural hills. Paid for by our insurance company that we were indeed lucky to have and we had managed to settle up at the cottage for what we believed a short amount of time before we could move into our new home as arranged.

The house with the fire would be restored and sold, we would never look back or relish in any of its negativity again.

Lewis and I had our obvious arguments and fall outs, mainly due to the stress of the situation we had faced and were still continuing to face. It felt like hell and all the while with a young baby under the wing, we found it hard to stay sane.

Sanity, insanity, profanity?

Either way we were struck and yet to be struck by a decision made by what some may call fate, God, karma, choice, definition, and for the ultimate sake of all of our lives.

Lewis evidently had had enough and used his new self-found anger, frustration and own self languishing torment, to torment me in turn.

Mentally, emotionally and finally physically.

Whether he choose to believe it or not, my husband committed a crime that affected our set up, our family, our love. All over in a quick, very much predicted, event. He put his hands on me after a small bicker yet perhaps just one time too many, and what was a probable build-up of emotion in him or perhaps the sense of control, he determined our futures in that moment. I truly did not want to think or believe what could or was about to happen. Slow motion kicked in and it felt as though he had me firmly grasped to him for what felt like an eternity.

Shock and panic, fear and terror, shot in and I was numb, cold, motionless.

I did not have the mental or physical strength to fight back. He was extensively overpowering anyhow and I would not have attempted it. After Ava May called out for her Mummy and placed a gentle innocent hand upon us, he finally loosened his grasp and I could breathe, almost. Once I caught myself, I ran out to flee from him not wanting anymore conflict or much worse to occur. I genuinely felt my life was threatened and with that emotion running loudly in my mind the police were called and within a maximum of thirty minutes he was gone. Arrested, defeated by someone stronger and fiercer than him.

How did he like being the one unable to fight back now?

My entire body shook uncontrollably for days, this felt like a death or worse, I'm not sure how to describe it, possibly as if someone had come in and murdered your entire family and walked away leaving you with a lifeless soul, ripped your heart of all its love, innocence and trust. Took away your future and shredded any form of happiness that may have come down the line.

I died that day, I died that night, I died the next day and night and day after.

I died every day over and over and over, until I didn't think it would ever stop.

I knew it couldn't stop in my empty heart and now lifeless soul. My life, my future was now completely and truly over.

I had my beautiful, loving and happy little daughter right there in front of me, she would help me to get over this, but even that did not help. I didn't even see Ava May, she was merely invisible and I had no love to give her, to care for her, to nurture her.

Terrifying and shameful thoughts flooded through my darkened mind, at one point I even considered giving her away to some other caring person, I couldn't even get my head around anything I wanted to do.

To be dreadfully honest, all I wanted was for that feeling I had to be real. I wanted to be gone. I wanted it to end. I wanted to die.

Certain people in life when tragic things happen or horrible circumstances come around to test them, well they play the game and they play it well. Me, on the other hand, I had nothing, looking back perhaps just a little too much had happened and maybe I was cursed, I always had an eery thought deep down all my life that since I got horrendously unwell back when I had not long left school, I thought then that someone most definitely had a voodoo doll, not just on me, but also one of my friends. We were not the most well-liked girls at school, popular with the boys, yet with the girls not so much. We made a name for ourselves and people were envious, that was a given.

What if that is the real reason my life had been so difficult, and terrible, and all the strange goings-on were specifically down to a weird creepy doll that an old school peer made to stab me in the eyes, back, heart and soul every single day for as long as I could remember?

Instead of getting myself together and sorting out mine and my daughter's life, I questioned whoever would listen at that time as to WHY - *why me, why has this happened to me?*

The answer, the truth and the shocking realisation was yet to come…

CHAPTER TWENTY FOUR

Dying to Move On

It is during our darkest moments that we must focus to see the light.

Aristotle

Emily

The sheer grief of all the events I had just been through - how could I begin, carry on, or even come to terms with it, or even understand it all?

The man I thought I loved had become the devil, yes in real terms, not just overnight, but to me at that unsightly moment in time he had appeared to change overnight. My belief was overly stricken, my daughter needed and wanted her Mum to be whole and pure, and to love her more at that time, than I had ever done before.

My home that I hated anyway was now completely gone and I was trying to come to the accepting fact that that chapter of our lives was now overwhelmingly surreal. Here I was, sat in a house that was not my own, a child who now had a single mother for a family, a mother that had not a penny to her name, a mother that could no longer provide for us both, and a mother that was facing the reality that in just four weeks she and Ava May would be homeless, with just a few bags of belongings to our names.

That was our world and we could either crumble and disappear quietly, or stand up and fight.

I chose the latter, only because of the empowering sense of adrenaline, cortisol and fight mode that were all kicking into my system like a high enabling, nonstop moving drug. Hence, I was full of energy, get up and go, the strength to simply get through the current events, not the future, just the present tense.

Don't get me wrong, I still wanted to be gone, for the ground to swallow me up - as clichéd as it sounds - I really did.

If the choice had been there to take the easy road, I would've ripped that ticket right out of the hand that offered it and I'd have been gone. Fortunately for me and my child, that option just was not there and that was in hindsight, a real honest blessing.

The days passed fast, extremely fast, I got by on my nervous energy alone, food was not an option. The sickness and upset controlled my appetite like a gun to my head. Eat, but you may die. While waiting for any news on my now ex-husband coming through from the police about his unforgivable behaviour, I stumbled; well, that's a lie. I most absolutely and deliberately sat myself down and latched on to his open laptop. The mistake he made was to leave everything open and running before he got carted off.

There I was, my heart pounding, I could physically hear every single beat as they all conjoined into one hundred million; I did not want to find a single thing, yet I knew in that crazy beating heart of mine, that all the things I did not want to see or read would be there.

As I trawled through the laptop's web history, I recalled that it wasn't the first time I'd done this as Lewis had lied to me previously about his addictions. Porn, of course. The first time I had discovered this, he'd shown me the full extent of his wrath and his hidden temper. Luckily, that night it had only escalated to raised voices, nothing physical - yet.

It was not taken any further as he'd apologized and I was hung back upon his little string, as he worked me all over again, like the puppet I was in those days.

That's how Lewis saw me - as an object - no meaning, just a thing he could play with or hurt mainly whenever he wanted or, most importantly, needed to, despite the consequences or destruction that may be caused.

In my case, it resulted in the savage, long lasting, mental and physical damage perpetrated upon my mind, body and my soul.

After I had trawled endlessly through the web history trying to find something more damning compared to the previous time that had only been a few months before, I realised that his email account was open. Yes, I ingested that fact excitedly, like a little girl in a shop about to find the toy they'd always wanted. For me it was an option I'd not had before - to find out the real truth once and for all - it that gave me a little skip in my step.

If I would've known what I was about to discover, I would've maybe waited, or passed up the opportunity completely, as I was not ready for it.

The emails really didn't show much and I found no evidence that would have set my mind at peace. I decided to type a few word suggestions into the search box. Bingo! As I'd expected, email upon email from woman after woman and, honestly,

God knows what, or who else. They all appeared and I went through them one by one, disgusting myself further the point of retching and hyperventilating.

This evidence gave me all the true details of the real man he was.

A loyal husband, hardworking and honourable man, a father, a provider - he was not.

A cheat, porn and sex addict, gambler, drug abuser, liar, disgrace, vile - he was.

Believe it or not, this actually hurt me more than any physical abuse or pain from him had ever done. I still do not understand why the emotional pain hurts the way it does, why the heartbreaks, and why the mere sight of such disloyalty cuts deeper and more painfully, yet it does so, in every possible way.

I never would've thought that he might be capable of cheating on me like he'd done, yet he did and it was unforgivable.

The hardest part by far was not being able to speak to him or confront him on what I'd found out. I decided to hold my cards close to my chest and to use this knowledge to my advantage. It's true what they say that 'knowledge is power' and a little saying of mine that I like to use in addition is: 'and power is key'.

Key to my new start, my new life, my new home; I just had to get there.

Days went by quicker than time itself and the next I knew it, Lewis was out of custody and at home, awaiting his trial for assault against me. The problem was he was out on bail for approximately twelve weeks which made things more difficult and uncertain as we were to move into our new home within four weeks. I didn't know if he would allow myself and Ava May to enter into yet another one of his properties as silly little old me had never taken my name off the mortgage to our second home, due to my being on maternity leave. He had me right where he wanted me or, as I mentioned earlier, right where he needed me. Just as I'd thought and knew, Lewis did make sure that Ava May and I did not get that new house, all three bedrooms of it, and it was such a nice house in another newbuild estate that I myself had chosen. Lewis liked to let me believe I had some choices in life to keep the game of the fool play out, right up to the limit. Facing homelessness and the very frightening prospect of just what the future might hold for my daughter and myself, I continued to read Lewis's emails and I kept notes of what was said from the lawyer to Lewis and back again, the house dealings, and anything else worth noting.

An insurance payment from our house fire finally came through, all £40,000 of it and the money looked so perfect sitting there in our joint account which was open and in full use. An email came through that stated he wanted to get all of the money into an account of his own to prevent me from accessing a penny of that or the sale of our home.

Lewis wanted to ruin me, good and proper.

Taking money was something I would never have considered, however, faced with the non-opportunity and lack of life there was for me and my baby, I chose the drastic option of transferring the entire amount of the money from the insurance, into an account of my own.

Gladly, I sat, pondering this matter for days, spending enough time to ensure it was the right thing to do and that we would be alright legally. My lawyer did quote something along the lines of *'taking that money would be like an atomic bomb going off'*, which I then laughed off. It created a few bombs as expected, though karma is a funny old thing, and certainly comes around to bite you in just the right places, and on this occasion a small chuckle was in aid of. I felt like I had won the lottery, albeit a small lottery of life and, in doing so, it had left a very sour taste in my mouth. Unlike Lewis, I am not a bad person. Quite the opposite, in fact.

I firmly believed that one of us must put Ava May, our child, whom we had brought into this world together, first.

While his parents coincided with all of his wrongdoings, helping him along financially, and all the rest, I dragged, pulled and fought to get myself and Ava May out of a serious muddy hole and, so far, we were about a quarter of the way out of it.

During that period, and I liked to call those times the *'absolute worst days'*, I would consume vodka, read numerous depressing emails of what next little act of revenge Lewis and his psychotic lawyer had in store for me down the line.

I lost weight, I screamed and shouted, I broke down every single day.

I would gaze out of the window on the busy road, considering more times than I can now recall the act of throwing myself in front of the very next vehicle as it sped along at 60 mph outside my then accommodation. Staring up at the sky, I'd imagine what it would be like for Ava May to grow up without a mother, without the truest person, the closest person to her, to hug, kiss, cuddle, support, teach and love her, because I know no one other than me who could've given her the life she needed. She needed her mum.

Instead I would think to myself, *Okay, maybe, just maybe, down the line… if that's the only option I have, then I may take that way out… But let's just see where this whole car crash of a life can go.*

Could you really repair car wreckage?

Could you smooth out something once it's crumpled and tossed onto the floor?

Could you smash a vase made of glass to smithereens, then glue it back together piece by piece?

The answer to all of these inner questions may be 'yes', but would those things be anywhere near the same again, even if somewhat a little different?

Some days I hated Lewis; I wanted to be in a room alone with him and a weapon of my choice. Other days I needed him, that is what control does, it leaves you feeling incapable of coping alone. It wasn't until he was gone for good and he couldn't get to me physically, mentally or verbally, that I actually began to repair.

First came the health differences.

The nausea vanished, the headaches left; the stomach pain was also gone, amongst other things. There were many times during that relationship when friends and family, the ones that actually stuck around, had questioned my health and symptoms and we had all joked, then we had simply put it down to me being, unknowingly, drugged by Lewis.

We never took it seriously as no one, including myself, realised just how bad the relationship had actually become, or how bad he was behaving, who he really was and what he might be capable of.

Then there were the long list of days and times I genuinely thought I was either crazy or being led to believe that I was. However, I had become certain that he was recording me while at work and also when I was home alone with Ava May.

I would have private conversations with my mother or friends around lunchtime of a particular day and later on, there Lewis would be, winding down at night after dinner, and he would randomly begin talking about the very subject that I had been discussing earlier with my mother or someone else.

He'd repeat the exact phrases I'd used - it would scare me and unnerve me.

Eventually I called him out on it as it had become such a regular event. Of course, he denied it, calling me crazy and '*paranoid*'. That was to become his favourite word of all time and I felt like I was being slapped over and over with it and that he thought I was '*paranoid*'.

However, I thought, what if he had been, and still was, recording me or watching me?

The day I discovered the empty folder on his laptop called '*Sound Recordings*' confirmed it was true, though due the file being empty and the computer's bin have been eradicated, I had nothing to go on and could only wait for a bug to turn up or fall out of a ventilator or a photo frame, then I would know for sure.

I pondered over the idea that it may be a spying app on my mobile phone, but I was just not techie enough to be able to locate the pinning point to nail him for that one. Instead I began carefully watching every little thing I said or did until the fire burned the house down. Whatever device Lewis had been using, supposing that he had done so, it was most likely destroyed, or possibly discovered by the fire team. Even then, I doubt that it would've been flagged up, as so many people were using indoor home cameras back then, as they do today.

The post arrived on a Monday morning after a long, quiet, uninterrupted weekend. It was now three weeks after I'd had to leave the temporary accommodation supplied by the insurance company who dealt with the fire. Myself and Ava May luckily managed to secure a little rented property that was let for six months to a year.

It came with many problems, clearly not the home of my dreams.

Lewis received the keys to our home, though he did not share any of the joy with us or himself, as he remained at a distance and was staying in his hometown with his parents. As for our old house that had been destroyed by the accidental fire, the buyer had completed and moved in with only half of the kitchen ready, which she'd agreed to finish herself. Life was slow, though I wouldn't say much calmer as the lawyers were battling on different terms between myself and Lewis, while we awaited his trial. I never enjoyed opening the post as people always associated mail with negativity, what with it usually being bills, demands or changes, come what may. Financially, I'd always been okay and stable before Lewis and I were married, then he rocked that boat so much that we were in the red most months. I could never truly understand why it happened, yet he managed to create it often and easily. He would come back from a shopping trip for groceries with one small bag yet had spent £90; I found this extremely questionable.

If a man wants to get away with doing something they should not, they find a way that goes undetected, always.

That Monday when I opened the post, it turned out to be a good day, as the post was positive. It was a change for the better and it was perhaps a new lifeline. In that post was a letter, a chance, and a road to who knows. It may still be rocky or hard, however, it was an option I was willing to take. We had been offered the chance to buy a house. Me, just little old me, an opportunity to get onto the property market. Something I hadn't managed before due to running a business and not yet having the years under my belt in terms of income and profit, then becoming a mother and being on maternity leave left me bruised and unwanted by any mortgage company. Yet here now was a chance. As soon as Lewis was away from me, doors began to open for me, lifelines started to appear and for the first time in years I could breathe just a little easier than I had done before.

I'm not naïve, obviously I understood that this next chapter would not be easy or plain sailing in any form. However, I was ready for the challenge and as if it weren't enough that I already had Lewis, his lawyer, and parents all on my case for one thing after another, I now had to deal with a whirlwind of problems and unexpected mini pop up bombs here, there and everywhere as my life at that point truly was a minefield; a designation and field where I had no armour, no protection, no comfort or solace.

Not even one person to help me mentally through.

It was all about the fight - physical, enduring, exhausting - yet something or someone dragged me through as all the while I tried to put up a fight.

I applied straight away for one of the five houses that were left. Nearly finished being built, they stood in a brand new estate, modern, fresh, glorious, and I used every stem and nerve in my body to feel the love, joy and appreciation as if I had already got one. It was not easy, the houses had many applicants, I felt worried and lost at the thought of possibly missing out. I had to organise a mortgage, solicitors, you name it, all was needed just for the application stage. It took weeks, it took sleepless nights, it brought me fear and happiness, it gave me hope and got me through some of my darkest moments.

Moments, hours, days where I would roll on the floor, crying and screaming, hurt, calling out in extreme physical, mental and emotional pain after all I had been through, the biggest fight of my life; I was still fighting to get to the other side where it were safe and peaceful.

Some days I felt as if I was almost possessed and needed the help of a priest to save my dying soul, to rid my body of all the evil it had found itself in contact with. The priest would bless me and protect me from this ever happening again.

I used the power of my mind, my thoughts, the power of the Universe above.

In the past, before I met Lewis, the faith I had was the Universe. That was my God, whom I trusted and believed in, whom I turned to for answers and for help. I always turned to the Universe, yet of course when I met Lewis he laughed, made fun, and told me I was mad and that there was no such thing.

Lewis was wrong, he was always wrong.

The Universe had gifted me everything I had before him. A home, a beautiful car, a business, money in the bank, and happiness, and Lewis took all of that away within a year.

Then it happened, the call came and also a letter of confirmation to say that I had been successful, I had been chosen.

That finally, I and my little baby girl were going to be safe, happy, free from him and all that he had done to us.

That we were going to get our happy ending…

Or were we?

CHAPTER TWENTY FIVE

Thus She

Paranoia is reality, seen on a finer scale.

Philo Grant

Emily

Over the weeks and months to come, I kept the house move and everything else top secret, mainly from Lewis. I could not risk any way of him sabotaging us and ruining the one good thing right now that had come into my and Ava May's lives, now he was out of it.

Lewis absolutely disgusted me at this point, I just felt ultimately relieved to be away from his control and the hold he'd had over me.

My mother was a great help with packing all of our things, she helped to keep my head mentally above water, yet I could still not let go of all the whys.

Why had this happened to us?

Why could we not have had the perfect marriage?

Why did he have to ruin everything?

Why was he like this?

Why, why, why?

It would all spin around in my head like a broken record; I was sick of listening to my own thoughts. My family were fed up of listening, my friends were bored of it by then too, and the people around me appeared disinterested, vacant and offered little advice. I think they felt in their realms that my storm had passed, that I was now out of the woods, that I could and should just simply move on and forget what had happened to us. I would never forget; I would never, not ever, look back, it was the biggest and the worst part of my life that I didn't ever wish to replay.

Then my head began all the whys, once again.

Why were people being like this towards me?

Why did they think I could just move on and suddenly become happy?

Didn't they realise I had just lost a life?

In fact, it had been a death, yet I'd survived.

Living on to tell the tale because, in their opinion, all I had now was a story. Well, how very wrong they were. I needed the pain to stop, I needed to look after my body and my mind. With many doors locked firmly shut, it seemed I felt lost, out of control, and truly I had no one to turn to and I worried I would continue to suffer with this pain and hurt emotionally forever, something I'd always feared and never wanted to happen to me, or to my child.

I bumped into an old school friend, we met for coffee, and we chatted long about our lives in those days and our awful exes. She made me promise I would never go back and that yes I may be hurting then, but that wound would eventually close and, perhaps more importantly, when I least expected it. My school friend was very much on my page, my wavelength if you want to call it. We were both big fans of positive thinking and that everything happened for a reason, whether it was good or bad at the time, there was always an important message behind it. She saw the pain in my eyes, I knew she could tell how I was really feeling as she looked deeply into them and I could feel the tears welling up. A reaction played upon her face; one I'd seen many times before.

When you tell someone a story, it could be a stranger or anyone really, but you tell them a story and they react similarly, responding with '*oh my goodness that happened to me too!*' And in that quick second, you feel a connection, a bond, and you know that this person really gets you.

That was how my friend reacted, then she responded as to how she had been there too, walked in my shoes, how it almost destroyed her for good yet it was her sons that got her through and still do. She was extremely happy now that she had finally moved on and met someone new, they had not long ago had a new baby boy and she was enjoying her life to the full. It was not just that which helped her, however, and kept her going, it was the help of a counsellor and a past life regression specialist.

I was enthusiastically intrigued and couldn't wait to hear the results of her encounter with Raine, the specialist.

My friend explained everything clearly and told me that it had simply changed her life, and her outlook. I was given Raine's contact details and I made a promise that I would get in touch to book an appointment. We left our catch-up there and I haven't seen my school friend since.

I heard since through another friend that my friend's newfound happiness and long-awaited 'perfect man' turned out not to be so perfect after all. The full ins and outs I do not know, however, I'm aware that she is now on her own once again, living, breathing and getting through her life as a single mother with her two boys. What I do know is that she is strong, she has healed, and she knows how to handle the hard times, she will get through it. Hope and new beginnings are more than likely waiting around the corner for her.

As for any of us, you just need to get up, get moving, and get out to walk around that corner, and you may eventually find what you're looking for.

I called Raine the very next day, while I still awaited the move into our new home. Raine was lovely, extremely pleasant and understanding. She arranged an appointment within the week and I managed to arrange child care for Ava May, as I felt this was the kind of place that I needed to go alone.

I had to do this for myself and I was right.

I arrived at Raine's home address as this is where she carries out most of her work. I walked up the steep steps and chapped on the door. It was an old-style knocker and I had a warm feeling about the house I was about to step into. Raine opened the door, or at least I automatically assumed it was herself, really at that moment this woman in front of me could have been anyone. Her mid-length dark hair practically verging on black in the exact colour, Raine had a wide smile that lit up her entire face. With her petite shoulders and thin build, she was small yet looked strong and well put together.

Even now and back then I still would get feelings, or as some would say vibes, from certain people or situations, and many people that I come into contact with can actually end up draining all of my energy from within, leaving me flopped, disinterested in life and even unwell.

I didn't feel that with Raine, not at that moment, anyway. You see when people are good, strong, positive, and have well energy they don't tend to usually take mine. The ones on the other hand that do, I call them energy vampires, and they can have a seriously detrimental effect on my wellbeing. I knew and still know this, yet I do not understand why I wanted all of that and more to change.

Raine introduced herself and shook my hand which was a warming thing to do, as well as professional. She then steered me into the front room of her home. Her house was extremely big, I would say on average she more than likely had around three living areas. The front room was cosy, warm, and somewhat old fashioned in style.

Raine was in her mid to late 40s and, from what I could see of some of the ornaments and objects within the space, they appeared much older in age and had perhaps been passed down to her from older generations.

Once we were both sat down comfortably, she explained a little about herself and what I should and could expect from her service, which was mainly that of counselling and past life regression. She then allowed me to speak for a period of time and before long, my tears were rolling and my shoulders were tense.

I felt emotionally out of control.

She stopped me right there and said, "Okay, we can help with this and we can control this and have you back in a better place, a place you will want to stay, enjoy and happily live in."

Raine gave me endless amounts of advice, help, determination, and positivity. It all truly helped, it twigged little thoughts in my head that I had never had before and it opened my eyes wide and clear.

"Empath," she said.

I suddenly thought, *Did she just say that or am I making it up?*

I was wrong, she did say it and then vastly went on to explain what it was and why I was one.

Basically, in easy terms, it is a person who has too much empathy for people less fortunate or struggling and so you can feel what they feel, think what they think, just understand a little too much, and that it is not a good thing. This made perfect sense to me as most of the people around me then and during most of my life had been this way, they were energy vampires - I did know that. However, they preyed upon me and my caring empathic nature. It, in turn, made me sick physically, as I've said before I knew that my well-being took a hit in just the energy stakes.

Now with Raine, I realised that I have always been an empath and this information took things to a whole new level.

I've always attracted people to me in this way.

Even though this was one of the reasons I'd attracted difficult people, be it in relationships or friendships, or with general members of the public, Raine made it seem very probable and she also made me aware that the people I had been dealing with in my past relationships may in fact have been sociopaths, and sociopathic behaviour could be extremely damaging to another human being.

That kind of behaviour can result in physical, emotional and mental abuse, which I had suffered at the hands of Lewis.

It got me thinking, was Lewis a sociopath and, if so, why?

The most important takeaway from discovering this was that, yes being a sociopath was and is an illness, however, there is no cure. Some people were born this way or developed it at such a young age and it was often too late by the time they reached adulthood to help them. Not only that, Raine continued further to tell me about the impact of his condition on me and she said my past life may well be affecting my life now.

I was shocked and unsure though I could see that Raine very much appeared to know what she was talking about and was very clear with what she was saying.

The only way to find this out for sure was to undergo a past life regression.

Past life regression is a form of hypnotherapy that has you somewhat asleep yet fully aware of your surroundings and you can stop the process at any time. It could take around an hour and you may discover interesting facts or issues from you past life that may be affecting your current life situation.

I felt excited and I was definitely eager to discover what I may get from the process. Raine told me that I could have it done during the next session and I happily agreed. I left Raine's home feeling a little lighter and more positive about the future ahead. A whole week was to be accomplished before I could return for the past life session.

A lot happened in that week. Lewis got let off with his assault charge and conviction, the judge decided to throw the case out due to him having a decent career, much to my lawyer's dismay and of course, my own. He was then able to contact me after twelve weeks of bail conditions. I was unsurprised to see a text message come through from him, he wanted to meet up to discuss our future and everything that had happened.

In my head I wasn't interested, not even one bit bothered, however, in my heart I still felt a loss and, unbelievably, a connection to him.

I had all this going on that I had to deal with. It felt almost like a job that I had to tend to on a regular daily basis. I had to ensure that I come out of this situation with what I needed and also with what I wanted to succeed.

Finally, the day arrived for my regression and after the past week's events, I wanted to experience this regression even more. I arrived at the house and Raine welcomed me warmly, as before. This time things were quicker paced; I think she wanted to put as much attention on this treatment as possible and she did not want time to control that. She had me lay down in the comfy sponge-like chair, resting my head back. Raine told me I could close my eyes when I was ready. All the usual hypnotherapy terms were used to help ease me down into the realm of the subconscious and when I was there it was bliss, peaceful, quiet and a place where I couldn't be disturbed.

I was then asked which door and so on I would like to enter, then to tell her where I was and I replied back slowly; just minor things to begin with. I told her I believed or felt I was in England and possibly, though I could not be sure, that I was back in the 60s-70s era. I don't know how else to describe what I was experiencing other than to say that it felt like watching a film with my eyes closed, yet I could see perfectly clear, everything felt real, like I was in the film, it was me.

During the hypnosis, while being in what I thought was England during the 60s-70s era I looked into a mirror. All I can say is it was not me who was looking back. I told Raine exactly about everything that was happening as it happened and she probed me to explain further who was looking back in the mirror - was it a male or a female, age, description and I gave as much detail as I could.

As is usual in this type of hypnosis, I was fully in my subconscious state, I could explain everything that was going on, yet mostly I did not remember a thing or just very little of the details. Raine took endless notes and replayed back to me everything I had said at the end of the session. She also tape-recorded it all with my consent, as proof I had said what she had written down. The end results were definitively staggering in every possible way.

What I had told Raine that day will haunt me and absolutely stay with me for the rest of my life.

From the mirror part of my regression which I do remember, I went on to tell Raine just who exactly was looking back at me in the reflection. I had said it was a female, similar height to me with shoulder-length curly blonde hair, she had a nice smile, blue eyes, sallow skin tones and was dressed in 70's styled clothing. She had a similar build to myself. She held up a hair accessory and was very attached to the item as she tried many times to place it into her hair. From there I was taken swiftly to a different setting and area, where I was stood on the top of a cliff; I could smell the sea air and hear the sea down below, yet I could not see the edge.

My body had a spinning sensation and when that stopped, I settled at a focused point which I felt still included this same female, now standing far back from a family who were enjoying a picnic on the grass-covered hill. There was a man who looked to be in his thirties, along with a little boy aged around six. The adorable boy had blonde hair like his father, who looked stern and rugged. He dished out the food and drinks at the picnic.

I wanted to go over, I felt a strong urge to be there with this man and boy. Suddenly I saw the female from the mirror reflection sitting alongside the man and child. The man and woman looked unhappy and were not talking to one another. The child wanted to run and play, yet the parents did not. Eventually, the female stood up and went to be with the child. When she held the boy in her arms, the man did not appear to like this.

As soon as I could catch my next sentence, I was hit with an extreme falling sensation, my whole body felt as though it was falling down and there was nothing I could do to stop it.

I could hear the noise of the wind, the air, and the crashing waves. I was then directed horizontally, hovering in mid-air, I could clearly see when looking back up, the man and his son looking down in horror, the boy was particularly distressed.

As quick as that, I felt a thud and woke up from the subconscious state back into reality, or as they say I was 'back in the room'. I began crying hysterically and felt overwhelmed by the experience. So many things rushed to my mind and Raine was surprised at just how much information I was able to receive from the session. We discussed the entire event and she ran over all the things I had told her.

I was in complete shock yet I felt a strange feeling of relief.

I left and we arranged another counselling-only session for next time. As I drove home, I ruminated over the hour-long film I'd just experienced in my head.

Was it real?

Was it just my imagination?

I could not come to terms with it, especially regarding how upset I felt as the strength of emotion that I experienced once I came back around, surely that wasn't over nothing? Surely that means there was some truth in it.

Raine promised to send by email the entire transcript she'd written along with the recording and that I would receive it within a few days. I needed to read it all once again for myself to try to understand it. Over the next few nights, while I awaited the much anticipated tape of my session, I found myself paralysed during sleep, along with having insufferable dreams, if not nightmares. I was consumed with thoughts and ruminations of what I'd experienced the few days prior and I guess my head was full up, and overly occupied with it all, to even try and contemplate any kind of normal functioning sleep. The dreams I had would play out similarly, they began with the little boy's face looking down on me, calling me, yet I heard no sound. Then I was at home in a house that belonged to me in the dream but one I had never been to or lived in. I dreamt I was her, going about my day-to-day life. I dreamt about Lewis and all that he had done to me.

I was always trying to escape someone or something, a dark cloud continuously following me around, I was always trying to find a way out and away from that.

Then I would awaken, dripping in a cold, shallow sweat.

Ava May would be crying in the room next door calling for her mum, she was needing to be consoled, soothed and put back to sleep.

Did I wake her?

Did my nightmare become reality for a second and enter into my actual life, that in turn impacted my innocent child?

After a long wait the post came with the transcript, along with the tape. I had very much wanted to hear the tape and I played it all through. Strangely, I could recall some parts. What I did not recall saying was where I was and whom I was talking to. Raine had written that I had specified I was living in England in the '60s-'70s with a strong connection to Dorset in particular, the cliff tops, and the seafront was mentioned over and over again as a prominent feature in my past life story. The little boy was called James, he was my son. My name was Diane Willington and my husband was Daniel. We very much loved each other though it had turned ferociously sour and in the end all we had left was hate. Even the love of our child was not enough to fulfil us once again. Not James, and especially not our next addition - the unexpected baby that was on its way. Daniel did not want it, I repeated. I sounded grim in tone and disappointment ricocheted throughout my being as I grew uneasy in body during that part of the regression. Daniel did not want me; I had said, or rather Diane had said.

I felt alone, unwanted, no longer needed, I had no way out, I saw no way out, I felt cornered and had no strength left in me.

Hearing and reading this left a shiver down my spine and a stomach wrenching disturbance. I did not know what to think or believe.

Could this truly be legit?

An honest account of a real probable event?

In my past life?

In Diane Willington's life?

I instantly had the urge to go on to the internet in search of my discoveries and to locate further any truth or possibility that this was in fact real. If it was real, if it had happened, there was and is the outstanding probability that James the little boy could actually still be alive today. I had read similar stories to this before and I never thought anything of it, people all over the world telling their parents that they had other mums and dads, or that they'd lived on earth before. I even told my mother I had another mummy when I was young.

Could this be genuine and happening to people for a reason?

There was only one way to find out. Hopefully, it would put it all to rest once and for all.

CHAPTER TWENTY SIX

Set Free

Only when I know, the truth will set me free.

Paulo Coelho

Emily

The internet search brought and came to nothing, after much anticipation, excitement, and if not stress, I let out a lengthy sigh from feeling aghast. I felt relief too though I still had a ponderance as to what could of, or still could be. However, for now, it was time to let it all go, I must try to move forward now one step and one day at a time. That line was the most hated phrase I would hear throughout my healing phase and I struggled on many occasions when people would tell me that. I would feel my insides grappling with one another and twisting with anger, fear, and frustration, all packed into one.

I didn't feel the urge to self-medicate or to meditate, yet rather I felt the urge to want to scream, to pull, to shove, to bang and go insane all at once.

I wanted to run and I wanted to hide from it all and wake up when the storm was over, not passed but when it was fully over and completely done with. Even now I still power on through with my mind as it dwells on the consequences and circumstances of the upcoming divorce, still continuing on to be a real thing in my ongoing life and future.

Although despite that, I am thankfully in a better place now. I don't know why but I suppose the darkness lifted a little, allowing me to see just enough light to enable me to take one step forward, living one day at a time. I laugh these days when I think about it because now I have left the fog and in front of me are many other women, friends, and colleagues of mine all suffering from the same abuse at the hands of their partners. I want and feel compelled to help, I truly do, yet I cannot, they won't allow it. They won't accept any kind of help.

They are scared, much more frightened than I was, believe me.

It saddens me and overwhelms me with frustration and pain that I cannot show them the way out, that they so desperately need to succeed at life - as mothers, as fighters, as survivors. When I stepped out of the darkness, out from the fog, into the pathway of a new beginning, a new dream opening up, I felt warmth embrace me, happiness succumbs me, and peace gathers me, wrap me up and hold me in its power. I like to think of it as a new power over me, however, this time one for the good and not for the bad like before. I most definitely did not get here alone and I'm still learning with all my might, focus, and determination. I will continue to learn, to carry on and to always take a step forward one day at a time. It's not always going to be easy, and all days are not going to be filled with love, joy and brilliant people. I will try though to take that in my stride and I think tomorrow will be better - tomorrow is a new day, a new light, a new step and a pathway to a happier future.

I only wish I could show and help the many others out there that are struggling right at this moment and who cannot think of a way forward, be it mentally, physically, or financially even. I get it I really do, there was a time when if I had allowed the thoughts to outweigh my decisions I may not be here today to tell my story. Yet, here I am and I will help if and where I can, and where I am allowed.

Numerous things have changed and probably the most important thing to have come out of all of this is the smile that is back on my little Ava May's face.

Radiating happiness, she runs with ease, she talks with grace, and she exudes love, positivity and free will. Everything you could want for in a daughter, in a child. It's how they should be, they deserve to be happy just as much as us.

It has been said before and I will say it again, a child does not ask to be brought into this world, though I believe that they pick whom to be born to, they choose life and the parents that will bring them into this world.

It doesn't make sense why some children come to harm or suffer at the hands of monsters that is true, however, we are all here to learn life lessons, or at least show others the lessons that need to be learned in order for the world to go around and for things in turn and by the hope of all involved, to get better.

Now I know that my lesson in this life was to learn how and to never give up, to always carry on no matter what hurricane came my way and messed my life up. I hope and pray that I have survived the last hurricane that I have had to endure and that now my purpose is to teach others, especially Ava May, how to do just that exact thing as no one for one second can tell me that she won't come across any difficulties in her life. I would not wish any of the things I have witnessed or experienced to come along her path, yet I want her to be prepared, be ready, to have supplies and back up opportunities, just in case she struggles to weather her storms, she will be ready.

To say what I went through as a mother, a wife, a daughter, a colleague, a friend, to all the people that witnessed me at my lowest points and my most excruciating times would be an understatement. They all now see me at the other side. It's as if I died and woke up born anew and ready for any challenge ahead. The strength I have now I sure hope never leaves me or fails me. I have faith in myself that no one and nothing can bring me ever again to that place I once lived in.

Things are so different and new, there is light wherever I go.

Ava May is succeeding at life and is growing into a beautiful and wise young girl. We have a gorgeous love-filled home, yes, a home where we all love, cherish and appreciate one another and where we are now. I am remarried to a wonderful man who loves me unconditionally, respects me in every way and treats me well. Just how any woman or person should be treated in a marriage or relationship, and I treat and love him back in the same measure. We also have a wonderful new son who is a very content baby and has slotted into our lives perfectly. Arlo feels like the missing piece of the puzzle and has completed all of us. The name Arlo is an English name meaning '*armed fortified hill*', which I didn't realise until after he was named. I found this to be quite fitting as if my past is linked to England and the Dorset cliff top hills and fortified meaning strength and protection. Perhaps Diane is still having an effect on me except this time it's a positive and helpful effect.

I feel Diane's story is at peace now as the land is laid to rest and that tale has finally been told.

My son is now with me to hold, love and protect forever and always.

I will not let anyone or anything get in the way of my love and joy for any of my children ever again.

Not in my past and certainly not in my future.

CHAPTER TWENTY SEVEN

The End

There are no goodbyes for us, wherever you are now you will always be in my heart and my soul.

Katie Johnston

Update
Emily

Months elapsed and I got over the situation somewhat, I say that as after all, I had learned, discovered and endured, now appeared and even felt no more than a past situation that I had been in and a part of. Today it is my story to tell and continuously learn from, accepting that was my past and no longer is it my present.

Most importantly, it will never be my future, I feel confident in that.

Although I was and am now settled in life and happy at where I have ended up, the curiosity and wonders of the imagination gripped me and got me thinking once again about this past life of mine and whether there were perhaps other ways to investigate its legibility.

With the powers of the internet, and the help of an ancestral advisor, we teamed up together in search of truths to try to put to rest the last few ifs and buts and, most obviously, the maybes. With Joel, my sort of detective of all things past life and the past, we searched into all the crevices to find any relation or truth that we could to pacify my story.

The results were eerily exciting and fascinating.

I had already worked out in my head that if Diane, whom I believe I were to be in my past life, was around the age of 35 in the 1970's and the 6-year-old son was that age in around the 1970's, then there was every possibility that the little boy could still be living today. He could very well be in the ages of between 40-50 years of age. He could now be married with children and if Diane had died at the age of 35 in the 1970's, if she had lived until today she would be around the age of between 70-80 years old, which then led me on to the topic of the husband, the little boy's dad.

Was he still living today?

All these thoughts and ruminations took hold of my sensibility and I truly at that point wanted, if not needed, to find some answers.

How could you explain to a potentially 50-year-old man, who just say had lost his mother to an unexplained death with a similar name, address, and lifestyle, that you believe yourself to have been that very woman and that she has been reborn as you, now facing a new life, world and choices?

Joel and I went on to discover a very old article about an apparent suspicious death of a much-loved woman in her mid 30's back in the 1970's era, located in Dorset, England, who had subsequently lost her life in an 'accident', which resulted in her coming off the cliff's edge.

Her name was Diana.

Unbelievably and disappointingly, no surname was found, however, they described the female as having a medium, slim frame and build, with blonde wavy hair. The news article tailed off with '*she is survived by her 38-year-old husband Daniel and her 6-year-old son James*'. The article also mentioned that Diana was with a child when she passed, sadly the unborn child passed with her. The age of the unborn child was not disclosed.

All of this felt strangely familiar and as if I had already read that story before, or seen it on television.

I felt it in my soul and knew then, mad as it seems, that there was every chance that what my regression with Raine had brought about was very possible and true indeed.

There were other avenues we could have chosen to go down in the search for the next discovery, finding James or even Daniel.

However, I thought quietly to myself, what would that achieve?

Ultimately not very much more than likely a very distraught man and father, who would never, not in a million years, be able to contemplate the information or come to terms with it. I felt it would be incomprehensible and unforgivable, with no logic, proper explanation or certainly no evidential proof and I could wind up looking like a fraud, if not worse. If it has happened to them and to me, I send nothing but love and good wishes silently in my thoughts and prayers to James and Daniel and I hope they have found some comfort in their lives after the passing of Diana.

As for Diana, I believe her now to be set free, alive in different ways, the story has been told if not recognised, and she will live on. Whether she has lived on in me or I have now surpassed her, I will never forget my experiences and circumstances.

I will never forget that niggling voice that said, *'Don't give up, not this time, not ever'*.

That voice, be it in my head or in my soul, said, *'Stay strong for you and for your child'*.

I'm glad I had a choice and I'm even more grateful that I chose what I believe to be the right path in this life. If it had not been for my past, I may not have lived to see my present and if not for the present, I may not have made a future.

Raine fixed something in me that I didn't believe could be achieved or healed, she made me understand that I was not just born this way and that I did not just have to simply put up with it.

I was a fighter last time and I have fought this time.

Now like Diana, I am free, I feel it in every part of my spirit, my energy and my body. I am healed, I am relieved, and I can continue on each and every road presented as I will never give up, the past has shown me that by far.

Most importantly, I will not give up now at the present time and I will choose happiness and make the right and good choices to ensure that I don't give up in the future.

This is no longer the past she lives with, it's the future that I and my family are going to be proud of!

THE END